STEWART FOSTER

We Used To Be Kings

VINTAGE BOOKS
London

Published by Vintage 2015

2 4 6 8 10 9 7 5 3 1

First published in Great Britain in 2014 by
Jonathan Cape

Vintage
20 Vauxhall Bridge Road,
London SW1V 2SA

www.vintage-books.co.uk

Illustrations by Maxine Foster

A Penguin Random House Company

Penguin
Random House
UK

global.penguinrandomhouse.com

A CIP catalogue record for this book
is available from the British Library

ISBN 9780099584193

Typeset by Palimpsest Book Production Limited,
Falkirk, Stirlingshire
Printed and bound in Great Britain by
Clays Ltd, St Ives plc

Penguin Random House is committed to a sustainable future
for our business, our readers and our planet. This book is
made from Forest Stewardship Council® certified paper.

MIX
Paper from
responsible sources
FSC   FSC® C018179
www.fsc.org

Max. Lobes. Tal.

Special thanks to Jonathan Bentley-Smith, without whose dedication, editorial judgement and friendship, this story could not have been told.

We look out the window, down into the yard where the shadows of children run and scream under the sun. They go in all directions, in straight lines and zigzags until they stop at the walls, turn around and start running again. We rest our head against the glass and close our eyes. Sometimes we wish we could go outside and join them. Sometimes we wish we could play soldiers, march in time, fire our guns. Sometimes we wish we had a tank that we could drive at the walls to knock them down.

But we can't.

No.

Because we can't drive.

—

And we haven't got a tank.

!

A bell rings. A hooter hoots. We open our eyes, see the children walk across the yard towards us and form into a line.

A bolt slides, a key clunks, the children shuffle forward. We stand up on tiptoe and watch the last one disappear through the door beneath our window. Even though the bell has stopped we can still hear it ringing in our ears.

We walk over to our bed, lie down, stare at the

cracks in the ceiling, the cobwebs that stretch from the light bulb to the corners. Footsteps and shouts echo through the corridors and halls. Our heart starts to thud, our head thuds harder.

This is the place where we live.

This is the place where they keep us. This is the place we have been trying to escape from for the last three years of our lives.

Because our dad has gone missing.

Yes.

He's gone to the moon and we've got to find him.

Who's telling this story?

We are!

Ha!

Ha!

A door slams shut. We roll over and face the wall and think about the times we have tried to escape. How the police always catch us. They ask us what's the point? What's the point in running away when we know they will always find us?

Because one day they won't?

Exactly.

So we have to keep trying?

Of course—

We screw up our eyes as a pain shoots through the middle of our head like a bullet from a rifle.

It hurts.

I know.

We put our hands over our ears and curl into a ball.

It's one of our headaches.

It's the first sign of our madness.

. . . What's the second?

—

What's the second?

The pain shoots again.

You know.

I don't.

Remember what Dad used to say?

Sporry wurry sputnik?

No, not that.

Don't talk when the planes fly?

Yes . . . and the third?

—

A sound grates in the middle of our head like someone with a spade is trying to dig us out from the inside. We press our hands tighter until our blood thuds through our palms. We know the third sign of our madness, but we can't tell anyone.

Except them.

?

Our readers.

What's the third sign of our madness?

What's the third sign of your madness?

The third sign of our madness is me talking to you even though I know you are dead.

—

We put our head in our hands.

—

I'm sorry . . .

—

I had to tell them.
It's OK.
But it's not really?
No.

—

—

We lie on our bed and wait for the pain to go away.

—

—

Can we show them our book now?
?
Can we?
I think we should just lie here.
We lift our head and reach under our pillow.
!
We've writ a book.
We've written a book. Our mum told us to write
it six years ago during the hot summer.
*We did it on the kitchen table every evening after we'd
finished tea.*
That's why it's crumpled at the edges.
That's why it's covered in baked beans.
Because you were too lazy to mop them up.

I'm lazy—
He's very lazy.
I only drew the pictures, he wrote the words.

—

Here's one of Dad's rocket.

It's not actually Dad's rocket.
But it's one just like it?
It's as close to the truth as we can get.
And that's important?
Yes. Mum said everything had to be true. She said our book should be like a Bible, and that we were her disciples.
She named us after them.
My name is Tom.
My name is Jack.
Tomorrow we will be eighteen.
Not me.
No, not you.
Tomorrow we will be eighteen and they will open the gates and let us out.

Chapter One

The moon hangs high in the sky and we wish we were
on it. That's where Dad said he had gone. It's 240,000
miles away, beyond the clouds, beyond the jet stream
and the atmosphere, but if we reach out and press our
finger against the glass we can touch it. It's smooth.

And it's cold.

It took Dad thirteen hours to get there in his rocket.
If we stole a car and drove at sixty miles an hour we'd
get there in 167 days.

But we haven't got a car.

No.

And we wouldn't steal one.

Do you have to interrupt all the time?

But—

It's hypothetical.

?

It means we can't actually do it.

*But I saw it in a film . . . a man, and a lady, and two
children.*

That was fantasy.

?

Magic.

Oh.

We think for a while without talking. Cars can't fly, but sometimes it doesn't hurt to imagine. All we need is FTT.

Flight, thrust and tragedy!

Trajectory.

Oh, isn't it the same thing?

No, not really.

But we're still going to find him?

Yes.

Tomorrow we will go out the gates without being chased. Tomorrow no one can tell us when to eat or where to go. We will be able to talk as much as we like, shout at each other and tell jokes.

We can run up hills and roll back down them. We can go to the park, play on the swings and roundabouts.

We can lie on the bank, drink beer, smoke cigarettes and get off with girls.

?

You can close our eyes.

Thanks.

A cloud creeps across the moon, makes us feel cold. We shiver, our breath plumes out onto the glass and turns the stars blurry. We wipe the window with the sleeve of our pyjamas, but the night sky has now disappeared into fog.

I think we should go to bed now.

'I wish you fucking would!'

We jump and turn away from the window. Martin Frost sits up in his bed in the corner, his eyes piercing through the dark. We don't like him.

Because he swears a lot?

Because he killed his sister.

He said it was an accident.

Ha!

What?

Jack, all murderers tell lies.

But he said she slipped on a banana.

He told me it was a pool of water.

It happened in the kitchen.

——

We don't go to the kitchen.

No. Especially not with him.

Especially not with a knife——

'Jesus, are you going to keep mumbling all fucking night?'

Sorry.

Sorry, Frost.

Sorry——

We put our hand over our mouth to stop our words coming out.

Frost lies back on his bed, pulls his blanket up to his chin. His feet stick out the end like he's in a mortuary.

What's a mortuary?

It's where you go when you're dead.

9

But he's not dead.

No, but we wish he was.

Frost clamps his pillow around his ugly head, rolls over and faces the wall. 'Aaaaaaarghhhhhhh!' he shouts.

Ha!

What?

You said he was ugly.

His eyes are too close together.

Like an eagle.

Like a bald eagle. They shaved off his hair because he had lice.

And he smells of fish.

!

But he does . . . sometimes . . . in the mornings . . .

But we don't tell him.

No.

We look back out the window, down into the garden where the shadows of tall trees crawl across the grass to the house. Everything that was dark has just turned darker. Everything that was cold has just turned colder. The hills are like clouds, and the clouds are like monsters.

I'm scared.

I'm excited.

We are scared and excited. There's a light on a hill with only darkness between us and it. It flickers on and off like a lighthouse.

Because we're on an island.

Because we're in the middle of nowhere . . . It's like Alcatraz without water.

What's that?

It's a prison in America.

The one with sharks?

Yes.

Are there sharks here?

No, only Mrs Unster.

Ha!

Shush! She'll hear us.

We stop talking and listen. Mrs Unster's room is below ours. Her radio is playing. She comes up and checks on us every night, just to make sure we are still here. She checks every room. The house is full of rooms.

And the rooms are full of beds.

And the beds are full of children.

Children like us.

'I fucking give up!'

And children like Frost.

——

Ha!

Our laughter echoes against the window.

Shush!

But can we tell them about the children?

——

. . . And the TV?

OK . . . We all argue about what is on TV. There's only one TV.

It's black-and-white.

One black-and-white TV, twenty-six children.

Not including me.

Not including us . . . We don't get to watch TV, the others stand in front of it and block our view. They say it's only the news, but we have to watch it to know when the next mission will go into space. We complained.

I shouted.

—

And I screamed. Aaaaaaargh!

'Jesus fuck!'

Ooops!

Sorry, Frost . . . but it was something like that.

It made our throat sore.

It made our ears bleed.

It didn't work.

They put us in here with Frost.

And I'm scared.

And I'm excited.

We already said that.

I know; sometimes it doesn't hurt to say things twice.

Like Dad did . . . Sporry wurry sputnik! Sporry wurry sputnik! Ha! It got on Mum's nerves.

Like you get on mine.

!

The wind blows through the trees, rattles the window. A draught tickles our neck and makes us shiver. We hug ourself and try to get warm, but our

blanket is damp and heavy and itches against our skin.
We yawn. We are tired, but we can't go to sleep because
we need to start packing. We turn to face our bed, it's
long and skinny and moves in the night.

Because I wriggle.

Because it's got wheels like the beds in hospitals. We
go to sleep in the middle of the room, and when we
wake up we're by the door. Frost can't get out.

And Mrs Unster can't get in.

It's our barricade, but she barges the door and still
gets through.

Because she's like an elephant. One day she fell——

We've not got time for that now.

Sorry.

We walk over to Frost. He hasn't moved for a while.
We lean over and hear him breathing, see a picture by
the side of his head, crumpled on his pillow. We try to
look closer. Frost grunts and rolls over. The picture
falls down onto his bed. We pick it up, see five people
sat eating fish and chips on a wall. His mum, his dad,
his brother, his sister, and Frost smiling, sitting in the
middle. We look at Frost, then back at his picture and
wonder how someone who looked so happy can have
turned into someone so sad.

———

———

We put the picture back on his pillow and creep
back to our bed.

Our clothes are piled at the foot end – three pairs of trousers with holes in the knees, four pairs of socks with holes in the toes. We reach under the bed, pull out our suitcase and pack blindly in the dark. We're not sure we need all our jumpers, they take up too much space and it's the middle of summer.

But it gets cold at night.

Yes.

We wear one, pack one and leave the third behind. Shoes are easier, we've only got one pair and we've got them on. We squash all the clothes in one side and look around the room.

Don't forget my crayons.

They're already in there.

And my Lego.

OK.

What about our aeroplanes?

They're under the bed.

But we're taking them?

Yes.

We reach under the bed and pull out a cardboard box. We put it on our blanket and lift sheets of newspaper out. Underneath are our model aeroplanes with drop-down wheels and stickers on the wings – Hawkers, Hurricane and Tempest. Sea Otter and Spitfires, Supermarines.

Fighters.

And bombers.

Our planes came in boxes with pictures of them on the front, flying between the clouds with fire burning from their engines. Dad used to open the box and lay out the pieces of plastic in a line on the table. He used to show us the stickers and put them in a saucer of water. They floated on the top and we'd pick them up on our fingers and stick them onto our planes.

We put swastikas on the Spitfires.

We covered the Messerschmitts with Union Jacks.

Dad said that was wrong.

He peeled them off and swapped them over. We didn't think it mattered. We thought they were just decorations to brighten up the grey. We didn't know it was so people knew who were their enemies and who were their friends.

We reach back into our suitcase and pull out a Lancaster: it's the heaviest and the biggest. We lift it up into the sky, stand on tiptoe and fly it from our bed to the door—

Oh no, do we have to fly the planes again?

I like it.

But we're too old.

I'm not.

We fly over Frost, back to the window, bank left and start the circuit again. The Lancaster gets heavy, makes our arm ache. We need to save fuel, fly higher, lighten the load.

Bandits below, bandits below!

We need to stop.

We only just started.

We'll wake Frost. We'll disturb Mrs Unster.

Who cares?

Our planes soar high up towards the ceiling. We bank and turn. Spin our wings and slide our tail.

Eeeeeeeeeeeeeeonnnnnng!

We release the hatches and drop bombs that scream through the night sky.

Boooooooooombhhhh! Boooooooooombhhhh!

They explode below us into fragments of burning light.

Oh shit!

That's a bad word.

Oh fuck!

That's worse.

!

Have we woken Frost?

No, we've bombed Mrs Unster.

Ha!

Shush!

Mrs Unster turns her radio up louder.

Under fire! Under enemy fire!

We climb high, bank left, bank right, dodge the white lines of tracer bullets, dodge the red splinters of shells. We clamber onto our bed, stall in the air, dump the last of our bombs and have a dogfight with the light bulb.

We should stop now.

Mayday! Mayday!

!

The bed moves, we wobble, the Lancaster veers out of control, takes bullets in its wings, smashes into the light bulb.

Oh no!

Oh fuck!

You shouldn't say that w——

'You noisy fucking bastard.'

He shouldn't say those words, either.

Bits of glass shower around our head and fall down onto our bed. Frost jumps up, thuds across the boards towards us.

'I'll kill you. I'll fucking kill you . . . Every fucking night . . . Every . . . fucking . . . night.'

We run to the window, along the wall, crawl under our bed. Frost crawls after us, tells us we're a bastard and grabs at our ankles. He pulls off our shoes, throws them at us.

Ha! Missed.

They go over our head and smack against the door. We jump on his bed. He jumps up, opens his arms like a bat and traps us in the corner. We curl up into a ball. Frost punches us on the head, sticks his elbows in our ribs, puts his knee into our stomach. Our breath shoots out of our body.

It hurts.

I know.

We want to cry.

No, we don't.

We jump up and push him against the wall. He kicks us, we kick him. He grabs at our face, gets a grip on our hair. We reach for his throat, curl our fingers around his neck, press our thumbs on his Adam's apple. His eyes bulge. We squeeze tighter. He makes a noise like a cat being sick. The bed moves away from the wall. We fall over the top of his bedstead onto the floor. We roll over and over, one moment we are on top of him, the next he is on top of us. Shards of glass stick in our back. We hold on tight, turn away when he dribbles spit onto our face.

'You bast—'

The music turns off.

We stop.

We listen.

We stare at Frost.

He stares at us.

We pant like dogs.

A door clicks open. A door slams shut. We hear footsteps land heavily at the bottom of the stairs, then get heavier and louder the closer they get to the top. Frost jumps up, runs across the room and climbs into his bed. We lift up our case, put the Lancaster inside and close the lid. The footsteps thud along the landing. A shadow stops, blocks the light under the door. We climb into bed, lie down and pull our blanket over our head.

I can't breathe.

Shush!

The door clicks open. We spy through a hole in the blanket. Mrs Unster's body blocks the doorway. The only place that light gets through is either side of her head. She sucks in air and then blows it back out.

Has she got asthma too?

No, she's just fat.

Oh.

'What you doing?'

—

—

'I said, what you doing?'

—

—

'I know you awake. I hear you muttering . . . So, what you do?'

We slide our blanket off our head, put our hand over our eyes to shade them from the light.

Nothing.

Nothing, Mrs Unster.

'Nothing . . . Always you say nothing.' She turns and looks at the lump that is Frost in his bed. He snores loudly under his covers. 'I hope all your mumbling not wake Martin.'

Frost rolls over, stretches and yawns. '. . . Uhhh . . . What's that?'

'He wake you?'

Frost sits up and rubs his eyes. 'Yeah . . . they did . . . He did . . . Always talking . . . and more bombs, Mrs Unster. I heard lots of bombs.' The whites of his teeth catch the light.

It was only Hamburg—

Shush!

. . . And Berlin.

'And still he doesn't stop.' Mrs Unster's fat sucks away from the door frame, shards of glass crack under her feet as she walks towards us. She stops and looks up at the light bulb and sighs.

'You damage again?'

It wasn't our fault. It was an accident.

'Always you say it nothing. Always you say it accident.' She stands and stares at us. We stare back.

We . . . We didn't bomb Moscow.

!

Mrs Unster shakes her head, turns away, closes the door behind her, then thuds down the stairs.

Frost sniggers. We hear the sound of trumpets, cymbals and drums coming up through the floorboards. They shake our bed, rumble through our body. It gets louder and louder until it feels like we are surrounded by an army of marching soldiers.

I think you upset her.

Me? It was you that said Moscow.

That's where she used to live.

She lived in Latvia.

Isn't that the same?

No.

'Bloody nutter!' Frost rolls over and faces the wall.

We wait for five minutes, then get out of bed and start packing again. We park the aeroplanes in the corner of our case, wedge them together, slide wing under wing until the tips touch the fuselage. We get out our rockets. They are easier to pack, but we have to be careful. Dad used to tell us they were more delicate than planes, that they were more sensitive to the wind direction and pressure. We know we have to protect them. We wrap them in our jumper and then put the jumper in the case.

Are we packing our book too?

No, we'll carry it.

Can't we read it now then?

I think it's too late.

It's not.

We walk over to the window and angle our watch to the moon.

. . . Ten to two?

Ten past ten.

So it's not too late?

It is.

What about if we just read one of Dad's letters?

21

No.

I'll get the torch.

!

We tiptoe across the boards and find the torch on the chair by the piss-pot. We creep back, put our blanket over our head and sit cross-legged on the bed.

Like we are in assembly.

Like we are Red Indians around a fire.

We turn on the torch, it shines on the cover, on the drawing of us standing with Mum and Dad in front of our house. Dad's stood tall, smiling with his uniform on, Mum is smiling, wearing a flowery dress, and we are standing in between them with our hair in our eyes.

?

What's wrong?

I don't think our hair was that yellow.

It was, people used to say you looked pretty.

!

They said you looked like a girl. Ha!

That's all right.

?

I used to tell them you were my sister.

Oh.

———

———

We hold our book. It took six months to write, but we have been reading it for the last three years. Dr Smith tells us it's part of our therapy, that reading about our past

22

might help us get better. He says one day we will write another chapter, when everything is quiet and all our headaches are gone.

Are we going to write it now?

No.

?

Because it's not quiet yet.

Oh.

We open the cover and flick through the pages. Some of them have fallen out and been stuck back in, some of them are torn, and on some of them the ink and pictures have started to fade away. We flick past our pictures, past the maps that Dad left us. The blanket weighs heavy on our head. Where it has holes, the wind comes through; where our clothes have holes, we itch.

I can't breathe . . . My asthma.

We lift the blanket, turn it round so that the hole we spied through is now by our mouth.

Better?

Yes.

Our torch flickers bright, then starts to fade. We shake it to make it come back to life. An envelope slides out from our book and lands between our legs.

Are we going to read this one?

Yes. It might be an omen.

?

It might have fallen out for a reason.

Oh.

We look at the envelope, all the corners are bent and Dad's writing is scrawled across the front. We remember the day we first saw the letter on the mat by the front door at the bottom of the stairs.

I couldn't stop my teeth from chattering.

I couldn't stop my hands from shaking. We picked it up, ran through the hall into the kitchen and gave it to Mum. She told us to calm down, that we wouldn't be able to read the letter if we didn't stand still.

I wish she—

I know.

—

—

—

We put our torch under our chin and open a letter from the moon.

19th June 1971

Dear Jack. Dear Tom.

Last night the sun burnt another hole through our window and this morning when I woke up all I saw were the stars.

Tom, you would love to see the Earth, it never changes shape and it is prettier than the moon. Jack, you would love to float, but you would hate the food.

Georgi says Boo.

Viktor says Hi and can you make sure you're not looking at the sun by mistake the next time we come around.

Got to go, the deregulator just went irregular. I'll write again soon.

Love, Dad

X One for Jack

X One for Tom

X And one for the piggy that got left behind. Ha!

We have read Dad's letter a thousand times, but it still doesn't help us find him. He was so busy telling us about Viktor and Georgi that he forgot to give us directions.

But we won't give up?

No, we'll keep looking.

Because he would have kept looking for us?

Yes. We could make cards and hand them out in big cities, search through the bins in back alleys, stick posters in shop windows.

Could we?

Yes, that's what parents of missing children do.

But we're not missing, he is.

. . . True.

We hold the letter up and read it again . . . Dear Jack. Dear Tom. Last night the sun burnt another hole through our window and this morning when I woke up all I saw were the stars.

We shake our head.

Is it one?

?

An omen?

No, I don't think so.

—

—

We fold the letter and slide it back into the envelope. Our torch flickers again. We shake it, but the bulb just glows orange and then fades away. We'll have to get some money and buy new batteries from a shop when we get outside.

We lie back on our pillow. Our heart thuds in our head. We take a deep breath and think about the morning when we get to leave, when we will say hello and goodbye to Dr Smith for the last time.

I'll miss him.

I know.

Can we come back and visit?

!

?

We turn over, face the wall and close our eyes.

Chapter Two

We can't sleep. We can't stop our legs shaking because the thoughts in our head disappear but keep coming back again. It's cold and we're shivering like we have woken up early on Christmas morning. We wrap our blanket around our shoulders and look out the window. The grass is grey, the walls are grey, the fields are greyer. The moon has fallen from the sky and we are waiting for the sun.

Today is our birthday.

Not yours. Mine.

But we can share it?

Yes.

Happy Birthday!

Happy Birthday.

What have you got us?

?

We sit up and look around the room. There are no presents at the end of our bed, there are no presents on the table. We never get presents. We never get cake. We never get to feel good on our birthday. It's just a day when we get older.

I made us a card.

Did you?

Yes. It's here.

We lift our pillow and look underneath.

Well, it was here . . . somewhere.

We reach down between the cold metal poles and our mattress and feel the edges of a piece of paper.

Got it?

Yes . . . This is our card.

TO US. HAPPY BIRTHDAY.
FROM JACK AND TOM

Do you like my sun?

It looks like a cat.

Oh . . . but you do like it?

Ummm . . . it's . . . it's nice.

A door slams shut somewhere behind us and the sound echoes down the landing. We fold our birthday card and put it in our pocket. A boy runs past our door laughing. We hear the sound of feet scuffing and another boy crying.

It'll be James Lewis.

He's always crying.

Because he misses his mum?

——

Because he always gets beaten up?

Because he's opened his eyes and realised he's still here.

We get up and creep past Frost. He's asleep, lying on his back, snoring with his mouth wide open. James Lewis walks along the landing towards us, his head tilted to the ground, water dripping from his pyjamas.

Shall we help him?

I think it's too late.

He stops in front of us and looks up. His eyes are wide open and shiny like a baby's. We lean close to him.

They'll get bored.

'Will they?' He wipes his nose on his sleeve.

Yes. They'll pick on someone else.

Because the things they do to you they used to do to us.

Cold showers.

Stealing your clothes.

Stealing your shoes.

Dunking your head in the toilet. But we're OK now.

Yes, we're OK.

!

We put our hand on his shoulder and he jumps like we are made of ice.

We hear someone shout. James Lewis looks over his shoulder towards the stairs.

Run.

Run.

'Why?' He looks at the floor – a pool of water surrounds his feet.

We want to help him but we don't know how. We think of letting him in our room, letting him hide under our bed, but they'll find him easily because the sheets are so small that they don't reach the ground. We think of hiding him under our blanket, but he'll make it stink of pee.

The shouts get closer, footsteps thud on the stairs. We watch as he walks down the landing, stops by the toilets and pushes open the door.

We step back into our bedroom and watch the shadows rush by.

Maybe they won't find him.

They always do.

Because they're clever?

Because all they have to do is follow his trail on the floor.

The toilet door opens, slams back against the wall. More shouts, then a cry, then silence.

—

—

The water pipes rattle. The radiators drone. And a vacuum cleaner whines as it sucks somewhere clean.

—

—

We walk over to our window and try to block out the noise.

A black car winds its way down the road towards us. It disappears in the fold of a hill, then comes over the top.

How long will it—

Shush!

The car stops at the gates.

Sorry . . . but how long will it be?

Not long.

Seconds?

Minutes?

Maybe an hour, then we will be in that car, going the other way.

'Ha! You've got no fucking chance.'

We turn around. Frost sits up on his bed, wipes the sleep from his eyes. 'Do you really think they will let you go?'

What?

'Do you really think they'll let you out?'

Yes.

Yes.

He swings his legs over the side of his bed, sticks his hand down his pyjamas and scratches himself. 'You've got no chance,' he says. 'They'll send you to the YMI.'

What's that?

Don't listen to him.

'They'll like you at Houndsgate. They'll love a pretty boy like you.'

What does he mean?

It doesn't matter.

Frost laughs, then puts his head on one side and listens to the thud of footsteps coming up the stairs. He swings his legs up onto his bed and starts to pick at his fingers. The room goes dark like a cloud has arrived.

Mrs Unster stands in the doorway. She shakes her head at the fragments of glass scattered on the floor, looks at us, then at Frost. Mrs Unster walks towards him.

'You OK, Martin?' she asks.

Frost shrugs and smiles at the same time, then goes back to his fingers.

'So.' Mrs Unster's chins wobble, she nods at our suitcase. 'Are you ready?'

We've been ready all night.

Mrs Unster shakes her head. She knows how long

we have been ready. She knows we have been waiting longer than one night. She knows we have been waiting for three years.

We pick up our suitcase and walk towards the door.

Wait!

What?

We forgot our book.

We go back to our bed and pick up our book.

'Buzz.' Frost makes a noise like a wasp. 'Buzz, buzz.'

'You stop!' Mrs Unster raises a finger.

Frost grins.

'Buzz, buzz.'

Why's he doing that?

It doesn't matter.

Frost bites a piece of loose skin on his fingers. We look around the room, at the piss-pot in the corner, at our blanket screwed up on our bed, at the window we have looked out of. For a second we feel sad, because even though it is just a room it has been our home, the place where we have remembered Dad, the place where we have thought about Mum, the place where we have imagined all the other worlds we would like to be in.

Frost sniffs.

We have sat on our bed like him and watched people leave. We have watched them go out of the door, into the car park and get into cars or vans. Some of them shout goodbye, some of them just wave and some of them laugh and give us the finger before they go out the gates. And all morning, after they have gone, we sit in our room and listen to ourself until a new boy arrives with a bag on his back and a blanket for his bed.

Shall we say goodbye?

No.

Why not?

Because he hates us.

It might make him like us.

It won't.

Frost sniffs again as we walk past.

Goodbye, Frost.

'Fuck off!'

Told you.

!

We carry our book under our arm as we bump our case down the stairs. We turn left at the bottom and walk along the corridor. The sound of clashing cutlery comes out of the canteen. Mrs Unster slows and checks her watch. We see steam coming from the kitchen, see the cooks standing behind big saucepans and the porters wiping tables, sliding out grey plastic chairs and putting out green jugs of water. We sniff, smell liver and onions. They're preparing dinner before they've served breakfast.

Mrs Unster shakes her head. 'Not now,' she says. 'You eat later.'

We smile.

Because we're not coming back for breakfast.

Because we can get food outside. Crisps and bread.

And ham.

And cheese.

I don't like cheese.

I'll eat yours.

OK . . . We can have a picnic.

Yes. We can eat without listening to anyone screaming and shouting. We can drink without bread rolls flying through the air and bouncing off our head.

Ha!

Ha!

We leave the canteen behind us, walk on past radiators, windows and doors, jumping over the shafts of sunlight that cut across the hall. Mrs Unster starts to puff as we turn a corner; we think of slowing down, of saving our energy, but we know how far we have to go, we have been here so long that we don't have to count the strides.

Fourteen between Dr Greenaway's room and Dr Short's.

!

And sixteen between Dr Short's and the Assessment Room.

———

Mrs Unster begins to slow.

We've reached Dr Smith's door.

She blows out her cheeks, reaches up to her head and adjusts a pin in her hair.

'Here we go,' she says.

We look at the brass nameplate on the door.

Dr M. Smith. BSc. PhD. Head of Neurology and Psychotherapy.

Are we going to say goodbye now?

I think so.

We like talking to Dr Smith, don't we?

Yes, but not today.

?

Don't talk to him today.

But—

Do you want to leave?

Yes.

Then let me do the talking.

I'll try.

Mrs Unster turns the handle and swings the door open.

Hello, Dr Smith.

!

I forgot.

Dr Smith is standing behind his desk looking out the window. 'Tom.' He turns around and smiles. 'I thought it was you I heard coming.'

We step inside. The room smells of smoke and polish and aftershave. Dr Smith unwinds a piece of string that's anchored by the side of the window.

'Lovely morning,' he says. The string slips through his fingers. A blind falls down and the room turns dark. Mrs Unster starts to close the door behind us.

Our suitcase.

Shush!

My Lancaster . . . your Spitfire.

'What's that, Tom?' Dr Smith moves across the window and lets down another blind.

Nothing.

'Are you sure?' He clicks the lamp on his desk. We look back at the door.

It's just . . .

'Go on.'

We've . . . I've left my suitcase outside.

Dr Smith smiles.

'It'll be fine,' he says. He walks towards us, stops, puts his hand gently on our shoulder. We smell nicotine on his fingers. He eases us across the room towards two chairs in the corner. We listen to him hum. He sits down in the big one with wings that wrap around his head, nods at us, then at the chair opposite him.

Sometimes we think he has gone to sleep when we're talking. We accidentally kick his shoe and he tells us he wasn't sleeping, that he just closes his eyes when he's thinking. He is the oldest person we know, he tells us stories about the war, about Doodlebugs and Zeppelins. He is so old that even he has stopped counting. He says his wife thinks he is like a tree, that you can tell how old he is just by looking at his forehead and counting the wrinkles.

Seventy-two.

But not now!

Oh.

'Sorry?' He scratches his ear.

!

We sit down opposite him. Our legs are shaking and we can't stop our trainers from tapping on the floor. We put our book on our lap. Dr Smith checks his watch with the clock above the door, then hovers his yellow finger above a red button on a tape recorder.

We grip the arms of the chair.

'Relax,' says Dr Smith. 'There's no need to worry.'

We breathe out and stare up at the ceiling. We have done this so many times but it still makes us nervous.

It's like my first day at school.

It's like a worm is eating through our stomach.

Dr Smith checks the time again, even though only ten seconds have passed since he last looked. We sit back in our seat and close our eyes. We have to remember to be quiet, do nothing but answer his questions. We have to remember that both of us can't talk at the same time. Don't we?

———

Don't we?

I'm practising.

Dr Smith clears his throat as he presses the button. The tape begins to turn.

'The twenty-first of August, ten thirty a.m.'

——

——

'So, Tom,' he says. 'How are things going?'

We don't answer. We know we don't have to answer yet. We know what we have to do. We have to have a routine: question, count to ten, think, count to ten, answer. It helps us keep things in order.

'So, Tom,' he says. 'Let's—'

Complete the circle?

!

'Yes, have you read another chapter?'

We look at our book. Every time we have to complete the circle, we don't know where we'll start or where we'll go, only that after half an hour of talking we have to return to the same place.

'Have you?'

We shake our head.

It was too late—

We read a letter instead. But we could read now.

We open our book. Dr Smith leans forward, puts his hand on top of ours.

'No, Tom,' he says. 'We're not reading today . . . I know what's in there. I need to know what's in here.' He taps us gently on our head.

——

The tape recorder hums. There are footsteps and voices out in the corridor.

Dr Smith looks over the top of our chair towards the door.

'Tom,' he says, 'we've not got long.'

Until we leave.

'Until we have to go next door.' He leans forward and whispers so quietly that we can't work out what he's saying. We shuffle in our seat until our head nearly bumps against his. 'Tom, how's Jack?'

Who?

Me.

'Jack, have you seen him?'

No, I haven't seen him for ages.

?

—

!

Dr Smith shakes his head slowly and takes his glasses out of his jacket pocket. He picks up a pen and writes on a piece of paper. We sit up straighter, try to read what he has written, but his writing is small and scratchy.

Still in . . .

Still in . . .

What's that word?

Dr Smith cups his hand over the page like we are trying to copy him. 'So, tell me what happened last night.'

Nothing.

Nothing.

'Are you sure?'

He looks over the top of his glasses, raises his right eyebrow. We know what he wants, we know what he's doing.

He's leaving a gap of silence for us to fill in.

But we won't fill it.

No.

'Tom? Are you sure you don't know what happened last night?' He clicks his pen six times. We can't keep the answer in any longer—

We couldn't sleep — I couldn't sleep. We tried to read, but—

'But?'

It was too dark.

'So . . .'

So we bombed Hamburg.

Shush!

'And then . . .'

And then we bombed Berlin.

!

Dr Smith shakes his head slowly and bites his top lip.

'Tom,' he says, 'you can't destroy everything.'

But I didn't start it.

'Then who did, Tom?'

Hitler did.

!

42

But he did, that's what it said in our encyclopaedia.

Dr Smith scribbles another note, then taps his pen on the top of his pad. We look around the room, at the cobwebs in the corners, at the clock on the wall, at all the books we haven't read on the shelves. We wish we could read them, Dad told us we should read whenever we get the time. But we haven't got the time.

Because we're too busy flying our planes.

Because we're too busy reading a book of our own.

The tape clicks and makes us jump.

'Sorry.' Dr Smith flips the cassette cover and turns the tape over. We get ready for more questions, but he just sits with his finger hovering above the record button. 'Tom,' he says, 'can you keep him quiet, just for a little while?'

We shrug.

I'll try.

'It's important. We need him to listen, not talk. Just for a little while. Remember, I'm trying to help. Are you ready?'

We nod.

'Just you, Tom, no one else.'

OK.

Dr Smith presses the button. He checks his watch, I check the clock and we wait fifteen seconds for the tape to wind. Dr Smith takes a deep breath like he is getting ready to read the news.

'Tom,' he says, 'it's been nearly three years—'

And now we're leaving.

'And the pills don't seem to be working.'

They do. They make me go to sleep.

—

But then I wake up again.

!

'Jack.'

Yes.

'I said I need to talk to Tom.'

Oh. But will you talk to me after?

Dr Smith nods.

'Tom.'

Yes.

'We're going to . . . We're going to have to—' He stops and looks towards the door. We hear footsteps and then two men are talking outside. Dr Smith grunts as he pushes down on the arms of his chair and rests his hand on our shoulder. 'I'm sorry,' he says.

We watch as he slowly walks across the room with his head bent down. He opens the door. The shadows of men grow across the carpet, with voices that turn to whispers.

'Five minutes,' says Dr Smith. 'We'll be done in five minutes.' He closes the door, walks back across and presses the stop button.

Is it my turn now?

'No, Jack.' He takes off his glasses and pinches his nose between his fingers. His eyes are shining with little bits of red in the corners. He shakes his head. 'No, Jack, we're finished now.'

For ever?

'Yes, I think so.'

He walks over to his desk and opens up his case. It's as battered and worn as ours. He rubs his hands over his face, then pulls out a little box wrapped in brown paper.

'Did you think I'd forgotten?'

We stand up and walk towards him. The box is shaking in his hand.

'Happy birthday, Tom.' He smiles.

We hold the box in the palm of our hand.

It's not very big.

Shush!

But it's not.

We shake it.

What is it?

'It's new,' he says. 'I'm sure you haven't got it.'

Can we open it now?

The door opens and closes in the next room. Dr Smith shakes his head.

'No, I think you'd better open it later.'

When we're gone?

'When I'm gone.' He puts his hand on our shoulder, slides it around the back of our neck. 'Tom,' he says, 'when we go next door, when Mrs Unster comes to get you, it will be best if you leave Jack behind.'

But I can't.

He can't.

'But you'll try?'

Yes.

Yes.

He walks to the door, opens it and looks back.

Like he will miss us.

Like he is looking at us for the last time.

The door closes and he leaves us in the dark.

We hear him talking in the corridor. Then the other two voices, then Mrs Unster. For two minutes we listen. We think about what Dr Smith said about leaving one of us behind.

We think about opening the box.

We wonder what he meant.

I can't get the tape off.

!

The door opens. We tuck the box under our arm with our book. Mrs Unster carries our case as we walk along the corridor. She stops outside a door.

Assessment Room. Session in progress.

She knocks twice, then opens it before anyone answers.

Mr Stride and Dr Watts sit behind a table in front of three windows that stretch from the floor to the ceiling. We've seen them before, once a year on our birthday. We first met them at Dunston's, then again at Downend, and now they have followed us here.

I don't want to go in.

But you want to leave?

Yes.

Then we have to go in.

Mrs Unster nudges us in the middle of our back. We pick up our suitcase and stop in the middle of the room. Dr Smith is standing in the corner rubbing his hands together like he is cold. Dr Watts and Mr Stride look down at the table and open their green files. We look at the floor, out of the window, up at the ceiling.

We hear the sound of pages turning.

I want to——

Shush!

We dig our hands deep into our pockets to stop them shaking. Our suitcase topples over. The room echoes with the sound of our rockets crashing into our planes. Mr Stride looks up and shakes his head.

Sorry.

We're sorry.

He stares right through us like we're not here.

A line of sweat trickles down our neck.

We feel hot.

We feel cold.

Dr Smith pulls out a chair and sits down. He nods at the two wooden chairs in the no-man's-land between us and them.

No-man's-land?

!

47

No-man's—

It's from the war.

The war?

Not now.

But—

It's the land between trenches.

But there aren't any trenches.

—

Mr Stride looks up from the file. 'Are you going to stay standing or are you going to sit down?'

We'll run.

That wasn't one of the choices.

Oh.

We sit down. Mrs Unster sits beside us. Mr Stride pulls his file towards him, shelters it with his arm like he thinks we are trying to read it upside down. But we don't need to read the file to know the name that is written on the front. It's the same file as last year, and the year before, and the year before that. It started as a single piece of paper and now it's a book. And we don't need to look inside, we sneaked a look once when there was a fire.

But we didn't start the fire.

No. We only smashed the glass.

Ha!

One day we smashed the glass on the alarm and ran into Mrs Unster's room. There was a cabinet in the corner. We opened the drawer marked D–K and found our file inside. It was full of long words that we didn't understand. There were lots of pictures: one of our house, one of Mum and Dad standing outside, one of each of them on their own, one of us sitting on the wall at the beach, and one of us with our body cut off and our name crossed through underneath.

We used to be Kings.

We liked being Kings.

But we like our new name better. Dad had tossed a coin in the sitting room to decide. Mum thought he was joking.

But he wasn't laughing.

No. Heads for Armstrong, he said.

And tails for Gagarin.

Mum said she'd had enough, that changing our name was the final straw. Dad told her shush, that people might be listening. But we were the only ones there.

We watched him flip the coin. It landed on the floor and disappeared under a chair. Dad got down on his knees, but all he found were sweet wrappers and marbles. His face was turning red and there were bubbles of sweat on his neck. He lifted up the chair. The coin was in the middle surrounded by dust with the head facing up.

Armstrong.

Yes, but he said it was best of three—

One of the men coughs. We look up. Little pieces of dust float in the air as the sun shines over their heads.

All we can see are dark shapes. Dr Watts points. Dr Smith turns a page. Mr Stride speaks.

'So, Gagarin . . .'

Yes.

Yes.

He shakes his head. 'Well . . . we only have to sit here and listen to your constant mumbling to know you haven't changed.'

We have.

I have.

We're one year older.

!

'But you've not actually changed.'

. . . I can read better.

Shush!

And Tom's started to shave.

I said, sh——

Mr Stride shakes his head again, then looks along the table.

'Have we got the report? Dr Smith?'

Dr Smith puts his hand behind his ear. 'Sorry?'

'The report.'

'Yes,' says Dr Smith. 'It's all there in the file.'

We sit and watch as they all flick through our file. Every once in a while they mark their place with their finger, then lean over and whisper. Mrs Unster walks around the side of the table and makes it four against two.

Our feet tap on the floor, we put our hands on our
knees to stop them.

I want to pee.

Already?

Mr Stride takes off his glasses.

'What was that?'

I need to—

Nothing.

'Do you need the toilet?'

Yes.

No.

He closes his file and knocks it on the table.

'So . . . now you are eighteen.'

He is.

I am.

'Do you know what happens next?'

We're leaving?

Dr Smith shakes his head. Mr Stride smiles.

I don't think he means it.

I know.

Mrs Unster comes back and sits beside us.

'You can't stay any longer,' she says.

We know.

We're leaving.

'Yes.'

We're going home.

'No.'

What?

What?

'No . . . you being transferred.'

Transferred?

What does that mean?

It means they're going to let us go.

Yes!

But then they're going to lock us up again.

Oh.

'You'll be transferred tomorrow.'

Why?

'Because you still misbehave,' she says.

We don't.

We've got better.

She shakes her head, makes her chins wobble. 'How you say that? I hear you last night. I hear you talk, I hear you through the floorboards. I hear you make funny noise. I see you smash the light.'

But we were only bombing—

I told him to stop.

'You see? Who you tell to stop?'

. . . Him.

Me.

'Who?'

——

Frost.

Good answer.

Thanks.

Dr Smith leans forward and puts his head in his hands.

Did I do something wrong?

'Stop this!' Mr Stride raps his knuckles on the table.

Sorry.

We're very sorry.

'Tomorrow you will be transferred.'

Why?

'Because you're eighteen.'

But I'm only ten.

They look at each other and shake their heads.

'Tom.' Dr Smith stands up, walks around the table towards us. 'Tom, we need to try something different, something that will take Jack away.'

'Alternative therapy,' says Mr Stride.

What's that?

—

What's alter—

It doesn't matter.

But—

We stand up, put our hand on our suitcase.

What about Dr Watts?

'What about Dr Watts?'

He hasn't said anything.

'I concur,' says Dr Watts.

What does that mean?

It means he agrees.

We pick up our suitcase. Mrs Unster goes to hold our arm, but we pull it away.

'Be calm,' she says.

Why did you tell them we bombed Hamburg?

'But—'

Why did you tell them we bombed Berlin?

We run for the door. Our hands slip on the knob as we try to open it. Mrs Unster runs after us. Her face turns red and a blue vein starts to bulge out of her neck. We flail our arms like an octopus. She reaches for our wrist.

'You talk. You damage. You misbehave.'

The door springs open, two men in blue coats run in. We barge between them, knock them against the door and go out into the corridor. We run down the hall, our suitcase bangs against the walls and our knee. The walls and doors pass so quickly that they turn into a blur except for the door at the end.

Hurry up.

I'm trying.

We run out into the yard. The sun shines bright and blinds us.

This way.

This way.

We run around in circles.

Men in blue coats seem to jump out of the bushes, hold their arms out wide like they're trying to scare sheep. We run around the side of the house towards the car park.

In here.

Where?

Here.

We crouch down behind the bins by the kitchen. Footsteps come around the corner.

'They wouldn't make it across there.'

We hold our breath, see the shoes stop by our side.

'In here.'

The bins are pulled away one by one until we are left alone against the wall. We wrap our hands around a drainpipe. They pull at our waist, bits of paint and rust fall down on our head. Mrs Unster pushes the men in blue coats out of the way. She screws up her forehead and stares into our eyes like she can see something inside.

'Calm down,' she says. 'You calm down.'

We try to breathe and talk at the same time.

We thought . . .

We thought . . .

Our blood bumps in our chest, in our hands, in our head.

We thought we were leaving.

'I know.'

She slides her fingers between ours. One by one she peels our fingers away from the drainpipe. We close our eyes.

To stop us crying?

To imagine we are somewhere else.

We should be in the car going through the lanes, grabbing sticks from the hedges, catching air with our mouths. We should be getting out at the main road.

Because we like walking?

So they don't see where we're going. We could thumb a lift. We could get a taxi. We could get on an aeroplane and go where no one knows about us, all the things that happened to us, all the things we are supposed to have done.

Are we giving up?

We can't.

Why not?

Because.

Because what?

Because they're going to take you away.

We reach down for our suitcase and swing it around. It misses Mrs Unster and smashes against the wall. The buckle breaks, the lid flips open and everything is quiet, everything is slow, as our rockets and planes fly though the air. We watch them climb high in the sky. We wish we were pilots, we wish we were cosmonauts, flying up over the walls towards the sun. We'd go up through the atmosphere, jettison the booster rockets, make ourselves lighter, make ourselves faster. We would keep going. We would never look back. But our rockets and planes have started to slow, until for a second they stop and float in mid-air. Their propellers have stopped turning, the fuel has drained from their engines, their tails flip up and their noses turn down. Our back slides down the drainpipe. Our heart is thudding and our head is howling as our rockets and planes dive like swallows towards the ground.

We slide down onto our knees and screw up our eyes. Everything is black, except for smoke trails screeching a line through the middle of our head. We rock backwards and forwards, try to make the noise go away. We hear the sound of someone crying, open our eyes and realise that it is us.

'Tom.'

We see a pair of brown shoes. Dr Smith crouches down by our side. We look up at him, he blinks, wipes his eyes with his finger. He reaches behind him, picks up our Hawker and holds it in front of us. The windows are misty, the Union Jacks are blurred like the Hawker is flying towards us through fog. We wipe our tears on our sleeve. Dr Smith puts his hand on our shoulder.

'Any damage, Tom?'

We take the plane and turn it over in our hands.

—

—

Dr Smith edges closer. 'Tom, is there any damage?' We feel his breath in our ear.

The Hawker has scratches on its wings and one of the tyres is missing but we think we lost that on its last mission. We check everything else is in place.

Propellers?

Check.

Rudder?

Check.

Guns?

Check.

Bombs?

One's missing.

Let me see. It's OK . . . it wasn't in the box when we made it.

We give the Hawker to Dr Smith. He puts it on the ground and hands us our Lancaster.

Propellers?

Check.

Rudder?

Check.

Dr Smith gets up and walks behind a bin.

'Tom,' he says, 'I think you might need to look at this one.' He hands us Soyuz 11.

Booster rockets?

Check.

Capsule?

Dented.

Not cracked?

I don't think so.

Soyuz 11 has a dent just above the hatch door. We open and close it; it is still sealed tight, no poisonous gases can get in, no air can get out.

So it's OK?

Yes, it's OK.

——

I'm sorry.

——

I'm sorry I bombed Hamburg.
It's OK.

——

We close our eyes, bury our head in our arm and try to block out the sun, and the sound of boys shouting and screaming, and cutlery crashing, and chairs screeching across the canteen floor. But it doesn't matter how hard we try to block them out – we can't because the noises are already locked inside.

We feel a hand on our shoulder and look up. Dr Smith kneels down in front of us with our book in his hands.

'It's OK, Tom,' he says. 'It's OK, we can stay here a while.'

We hear the shuffle of shoes. Dr Smith looks back over his shoulder as Mrs Unster and the men in blue coats move away.

——

——

I'm sorry.

——

I'm sorry I bombed Berlin.
It's not your fault.

——

It's not our fault. It's not our fault we're here, it's not Dr Smith's fault either. We didn't know it would be like this. We wouldn't have bombed Berlin if we thought it was going to start a war.

Dr Smith puts our book on our lap. We sniff and shake our head as he gently places his hand on our shoulder.

'It's OK, Tom,' he whispers. 'Just read . . . You have to keep reading.' He opens our book. His finger shakes as he points at the top of a page. 'There,' he says. 'Start there.'

We blink, try to read, but the words and pictures are blurred like they have been splattered by rain. We wipe our tears on our arm. Dr Smith sits down next to us against the wall. We feel his body against ours as he takes a deep breath.

'Just read, Tom. Just read.'

The sun comes out, shines over the wall, across the car park onto the bins and all the things in this place that we thought we'd left behind.

Dr Smith taps the page.

We look down at our book and read about the last summer when we were home.

Summer 1971

It was hot, but I was cold the day after Jack died. I was staying with Auntie Jean. She wasn't a real auntie, she was just a neighbour who used to come round our house a lot and talk to Mum. She was old and said the same things over and over again about her husband, Eric. Eric was a policeman and he was dead.

But we didn't kill him.
No.
And we—
Are you going to interrupt all the time?

—

—

Sorry.

—

—

I wasn't sure how long I was going to stay with her. She said it depended on the authorities, but I thought it was because she wasn't sure if there was enough room for me to live amongst all her newspapers. They were piled high in every room I was allowed in and even higher in the ones I wasn't. She spent all day in her sitting room reading them, tapping her foot to the songs on the radio. Since her Eric had died, Auntie Jean couldn't afford a telly.

I stood at the window and watched the firemen carry their ladders away from my house, across the path to the fire engines parked on the kerb. They strapped them to the top, got down and turned the crank. The hoses snaked away through the grass with water spurting from their nozzles.

Auntie Jean put her hand on my shoulder, moved her fingers up and down like she was playing the piano. The paperboy walked along the path with his head down, reading the front page. He stopped and looked up at my house. Auntie Jean's fingers wriggled like spiders.

'Hurry up. Hurry up.'

The paperboy folded the paper like he had heard her, and Auntie Jean rushed out into the hall. I had only been with her for one day but already I knew that reading about other people's lives was the best part of hers.

She came back in, sat down in her chair and, while I watched the firemen lift the covers from the drains and brush the water away, she sat behind me making tutting noises like a rabbit munching on a cabbage.

'What is it?' I asked.

She looked over the top of her paper.

'Nothing,' she said. She closed the paper and folded it in half.

'Show me,' I said.

'It's nothing . . . really . . . Gosh . . . is that the time already?' She turned the radio off, tucked the paper under her arm and went into the kitchen.

Outside the firemen were climbing into their cabs and closing the doors. The engines started to rumble and the rumble rattled the windows. I rested my head against the glass like I did on the bus. My head droned, my teeth started to vibrate. Smoke blew out the exhausts and I watched as the fire engines pulled away. They went up to the top of the hill, turned around and came back down again. At the end of the road I saw their brake lights shine bright, then disappear.

I was alone, all I could hear was the tick of the clock and a high-pitched whine in my head.

A group of people huddled together outside in the road: Mr Thomas, Mrs Holloway and Mrs Green – people I'd waved at but never spoken to. Three more people walked slowly along the pavement towards them: a man with a black dog, a lady with a shopping bag, a girl with a skipping rope – people I'd never seen. They stood together in a circle with their arms folded, heads nodding, fingers pointing in the direction of my house. Then they saw me looking and one by one they disappeared.

My head was heavy and fuzzy like it wasn't connected to my body. I found myself floating through Auntie Jean's hallway and out of her front door.

The sun was right above me and shone bright, but all I could see were circles of purple and black in front of my eyes. I walked up her front path and headed up our hill, but I had only got halfway before I heard a whining noise and realised it was me. I turned around and looked down at our house. Our gate had fallen down and the garden fence had gone and the path led

63

to a black hole that used to be our front door. All the windows were black, and where they were not black they were smashed. They stared at me with dirty smoke lines pulling like eyebrows up to the roof. And no matter how long I looked, how hard I stared back, I could not see my reflection or anyone else inside. I felt chicken bumps on my skin. The newspapers said it was the hottest summer but no matter how much I hugged myself I couldn't get warm.

I didn't want to go back down but I knew I couldn't stay staring at our house all day. Auntie Jean came out and met me on the path that joined our house to hers. She put her arm around me and looked at me with her head on one side like a dog.

'Oh, my love,' she said. 'I wondered where you'd gone.' I shivered like there was snow in my veins. She hugged me tighter, rubbed my arms so fast she gave me a Chinese burn. She put her head on my shoulder, I put mine on hers. She used to be taller than me, but now we were the same size. We used to stand, back to back, like I did with Jack. When I was nine I was up to her shoulders, when I was eleven I was up to her earlobes. I didn't know it was because she was shrinking as quickly as I grew.

We looked back at our houses. Auntie Jean shook her head. I could tell she was wondering how the fire hadn't burned through our walls and into hers.

She let go of me. She had tears magnified by her glasses that bulged out of her eyes and glistened on her cheeks. I shivered again.

'It's the shock,' she said. 'I had the same with my Eric.'

I felt a lump in my throat, so big I couldn't speak or breathe. I knew Auntie Jean was only trying to be kind, I knew she thought it would help, but her Eric and Jack dying wasn't the same. Her Eric was ninety-two, Jack was only ten.

I went to bed, but I should have been outside climbing the hill with Jack, not trying to sleep in my football kit in the middle of the afternoon. I lay and stared up at the ceiling. Pictures of Jack and ambulances and fire engines flashed through my head. And when I turned over I could see them doing exactly the same. I remembered what Mum said, that sometimes writing things down made her feel better. I picked up a pen and our book and tried to write what had happened. But the ambulances kept crashing, the fire-engine lights kept flashing and our house kept burning and in the middle of the rubble and metal I kept seeing Jack.

I soon gave up. If I couldn't write our book I had to write something else.

I crept down the stairs, looked through a crack in the door. Auntie Jean was squinting through her glasses, knitting at the end of the sofa.

I went into the room.

'I want to write an obituary,' I said.

'Tom!' Her needles dropped into her lap. A ball of blue wool fell off the edge of the settee and rolled across the floor. Auntie Jean put her hand on her heart. 'For a little boy you're very quiet on the stairs.'

I told her I was sorry, that everything seemed so quiet, that even the sound of my own voice seemed to make me jump since Jack had died. I picked up the ball of wool and gave it to her. She moved a knitting pattern out of the way and I sat down beside her.

'So, my love,' she said. 'What was it you wanted?'

'I want to write an obituary,' I said. 'But I don't know what to write.'

She put her arm around me.

'It's Deaths,' she said. 'Next year you write the obituary, this year it goes in the column titled Deaths.'

I screwed up my eyes, my heart bumped hard and my throat throbbed and ached. I started to unfold the piece of paper and showed her this:

Auntie Jean shook her head.

'I don't think they'll take pictures, my love.'

We sat in silence and listened to the putt-putt-putt sound of Mr Green's lawnmower in the distance. Auntie Jean sniffed, reached up under the sleeve of her dress like she was trying to scratch an itch. A tear ran down her nose and got stuck on the rim of her glasses. I saw my reflection in them: my blond hair, my brown skin, my red eyes, my Arsenal football shirt. I leant in closer, felt hot and cold at the same time. I tried to swallow but wanted to be sick, because where Jack always used to be sitting in his Chelsea kit there was now an empty space.

'Oh, Tom,' she said. 'I miss him.'

'Me too,' I said.

She wiped her nose on a tissue. 'Oh, bless you . . . and you didn't even know him.'

'He was my brother.'

'Oh,' she said. 'I meant my Eric.'

She took off her glasses, blew on them and wiped them on her dress. I looked down at my piece of paper; if I didn't get started on my writing soon, Jack would have turned to worms. I felt a nudge in my ribs. Auntie Jean was smiling.

'Silly us,' she said. 'I'll help you, I did one for my Eric. You can copy it.'

I told her I thought I should write my own, that I didn't want to cheat. She said it would be OK as long as I changed the names. She looked down the side of the settee, said she was sure it was there somewhere.

I picked up the paper on the table.

'Is it in here?' I asked.

Auntie Jean turned round quick like I'd shot her with my spud-gun. 'Oh no, not that one.' She took the paper out of my hand and handed me another. 'And take this,' she said, handing me a red pen she used for crosswords.

I went back upstairs and laid the paper on the floor. There was a picture of an aeroplane with a bent nose on the front and a headline – CONCORDE FLIES SUPERSONIC. I thought of Dad, and Jack, and one of our days at the airfield, when we watched the sky and Jack got sunburnt. Dad said Concorde was one of the fastest planes in the world, that it would make a noise when it broke the sound barrier. We'd stayed there all day, drinking

67

orange juice, eating sandwiches until it got cloudy. We never did get to see Concorde, but at least we heard the bang.

I opened the paper and flicked through to the Deaths: Henry Booker is going to be buried at St Mary's Church at ten o'clock. All his friends are invited as long as they don't take flowers. He's only been gone two days but his wife Florrie is missing him already.

I didn't know what to write about Jack. It didn't seem right to say he was only loved by his brother. I thought about giving him an extended family, a doting auntie or an upset uncle. But there were no others.

I ran my finger down the page, through all the Alfs, Berts and Cyrils. They were all loving husbands and grandads who'd died after long illnesses. They all seemed so old and so dead, and in just thirty words their lives read exactly the same. Nobody young had died on that day.

I picked up the pen and started to write.

Jack—

The pen pierced through to the carpet. I folded the page and tried again. I added *Missing you,* then immediately scratched it out.

'Can I help?'

My pen jerked across the paper. I looked around the room. A laugh like a machine gun popped off in my head.

I heard the voice again. I looked up and saw Jack smiling, swinging his legs on the bed.

'Jack?'

'That's me,' he said.

I closed my eyes, felt my heart bump through my body. I knew this wasn't right, I knew Jack was dead, but when I opened my eyes he was still there.

'What are you doing?' he asked.

I lifted up my pen.

'I'm . . . I'm . . . aaaah . . . I'm writing,' I said.

'Our book?'

'No. I'm writing . . . I'm writing a death.'

'A death?'

'Yes,' I said. 'It's what you write when people are dead.'

'Who's dead?'

—

'Who's dead?'

I looked at my writing and slowly slid my thumb over his name.

'. . . A friend,' I said.

He pushed out his bottom lip and pretended to be sad for a dead friend I didn't have. I smiled, he smiled back and asked if we could go out and play. I said I was busy. He swung his feet faster, seemed to be happy. I thought it was weird that after what had happened to him he didn't seem to be scared.

'What can I do then?'

I picked our book up off my bed.

'You could write a chapter,' I said.

'I've got nothing to write about.'

'Are you sure? You haven't been floating . . . seen any bright lights?'

He looked at me like I had gone nuts.

'It was Dad that went to the moon, not me.'

'Draw a picture then.'

He took my pen, but the face that had looked so happy now looked like it was going to cry. He held up his hands up and showed me his fingers. They were black with purple tips like sticks of liquorice. He picked at the tops, held them under his nose and sniffed.

'Tom?'

'What?'

'Why do I smell of burnt toast?'

Chapter Three

We lie on our bed and look up at all the cracks in the ceiling, all the damp patches of plaster that have crumbled away. Mrs Unster is downstairs. All the doctors have got in their cars and left us behind. We shouldn't be here. We should be the other side of the gates, running along the road. We didn't think we would ever lie in this bed again.

—

—

We try to speak. We try to breathe, but there is a lump in our throat that is so big that no matter how many times we try to swallow it, it won't go away.

But we're not crying.

No.

Our mouth is dry and our stomach rumbles. We've missed tea and they won't bring us supper. We think about the YMI. We don't know what it's like but we have heard stories about people being beaten.

Do we have to think about that?

Sorry, but we have to tell people what it's like. We

71

have to tell them that it's a big house with black windows with big rooms that people go into but never come out of.

Like in cartoons?

?

Scooby-Doo.

Yes, except the house is full of young men and not ghosts.

We wrap our arms tight around our body and close our eyes. It has been a long time since we have been moved, it has been a long time since we packed our bags and went to live with strangers. We think of all the houses we have been taken to, all the hands we have held, all the paths we have walked up, all the doors we have knocked on and the more we think, the more we realise that all the places we have ever been to have all looked the same. Grey roofs, grey doors, grey walls. Black windows that we waved out of even though we knew it was too dark to see in. The only thing that ever changed were the names.

Hill House.

Huntingdon.

Kilmersdon.

Valley View. Mrs Foulks, Mrs Hunter, Mrs Drummond.

——

'Hello, my name is Mrs Drummond.'

Do we have to do that now?

. . . 'Hello, my name is——'

'Hello Mrs Drummond.'

Ha!

!

'I've been expecting you. You must be Tom.'

'Yes . . . and this is Jack.'

'I'm sorry, dear, I can't hear.'

'This is Jack.'

'Umm . . . of course . . . Hello Jack.'

I think you can stop doing the voice now.

Oh.

We close our eyes. We smell damp mixed with soap, hear the snap of a towel and a scream. Our head is buried deep in the pillow but we can still hear the gargle of water trickling through the drains. We need to be quiet to give ourself space to think, because tomorrow will be different, tomorrow there won't be a Mrs Hunter or a Mrs Foulks or a Mrs Drummond. Tomorrow we won't be locked up with boys. Tomorrow we will be locked up with men.

—

—

We roll over and face the wall. Three names and dates are scratched on the wall – Simon West, Steve Russett, Dan Parnell – all of them were here, all of them have gone, but we only know when, not where. We reach out and start to scratch our name on the wall. Little pieces of paint fall onto our bed. Our finger tickles and hurts at the same time.

Like pebbles on our feet.

Like chalk on a board.

We start to scratch the letter J. The straight line is easy but we get stuck on the curve.

It's a good job we've got sharp nails.

It's a good job we've got short names.

Ha!

Ha!

When did we arrive?

I think you should know.

?

1973. After Skylab started orbiting the Earth, before Mars 5 left for Mars.

After Mr Morrison, before Mrs Brimble.

I think we should concentrate on what's important.

But Mrs Brimble said she was important.

She said she specialised in difficult children.

But we weren't difficult.

Well . . . we were . . . just a little bit.

She said she had a bungalow with lots of rooms and a big garden.

We asked her if it had a wire fence.

We asked her if it had walls.

She smiled. We liked her.

She said we could go and live with her and her husband . . . and her dog . . . and her rabbit.

We told her we didn't like dogs.

We told her that we did.

She said she didn't understand, then walked out the door backwards.

She said she'd come back and collect us in a week.

We waited forty-five days.

We tried to escape in the laundry van.

They caught us and put us in isolation.

Then they let us back out.

Then Mrs Brimble came back for us.

But she took Billy Evans instead!

——

——

We look at our writing on the wall.

Jack and Tom Gagarin were here
1973–1976

The door swings open and makes us jump. We look over our shoulder. Frost stands in the door with his pants on, his white skin still shiny from the showers. He walks over to his bed and looks under his pillow.

'Have you touched it?'

——

——

Frost nudges the picture straight with his finger and puts the pillow back on top.

We look back at the wall.

'What are you doing?'

We feel him walk towards us.

'I said, what are you doing?'

Ignore him.

OK.

We put our hand over our names.

Frost's shadow grows big on the wall.

'Let me see. Let me see what you've written.'

Nothing.

!

He smacks his arm down on ours and knocks our hand away.

'Two tossers were here for too fucking long . . . Ha! Missing you already.'

He pokes us in the stomach.

'So, was I right then? You're leaving, you're going to the YMI?'

We stare at the wall. Frost bends down and starts to screw his finger into our ear.

'Was I right, dumbfuck?'

Yes.

'Ha!'

He jabs us in the back.

Are we going to fight?

No.

I don't want to fight.

We won't.

'Ha! Still fucking mumbling . . . It won't do you any good where you're going.'

Has he been there?

No, he only knows the same stories as us.

And they're not true?

No.

'Yes they are.' Frost sits on our bed, bounces up and down, then smiles like he wants to be our friend. 'All the stories are true. My brother told me.'

Have you got a brother too?

'Yes.'

Has he got a brother?

No, just a dead sister.

'What did you say about my sister?'

Nothing.

Nothing.

'What did you say?' He leans in closer and knocks us on the head with his knuckles. 'Hello . . . hello. Jesus, how many little fuckers have you got in there?'

Just me.

Just him.

'You're mad.'

Dr Smith gave us a book about mad people.

'Eh!'

Not now.

Dr Smith gave us a book about mad people.

Dr Smith gave us a book about Van Gogh.

He cut off his ear.

He painted pictures of sunflowers.

He couldn't stick it back on.

He sent letters to his brother, and his brother locked him away.

Like me.

Like you.

Like us.

'Who gives a fuck?' Frost shakes his head like we are inside it.

What was your sister's name?

'I said don't talk about my sister!' He jumps on top of us, pins our shoulders to the bed. We kick our legs and try to knock him off. He slides forward, clamps his knees either side of our head. His mouth moves, but all we can hear are mumbles.

Like we are deaf.

Like he is talking underwater.

He grins and licks his fingers, then points them at us like he's going to poke us in the eyes.

Get lost.

Fuck off!

We wriggle again.

Frost laughs then slides his fingers either side of our head and digs them deep into our temples.

'Buzz. Buzz.'

Why does he keep—

It doesn't—

'Buzz. Buzz.'

Our blood starts to thud. Frost presses his fingers like he's drilling two holes that will meet in the middle. We kick our legs harder.

Fuck off, Frost, he doesn't know.

What don't I know?

We knee Frost in the back. He grunts and falls off the bed onto the floor. We jump on top of him, try to grab his arms, try to make him submit, but his body is still slippery from the soap.

What don't I know?

We put our hands round his neck. His laughter vibrates through our fingers.

Don't let go.

What don't I know?

It doesn't matter.

'They're going to—'

We squeeze tighter. Frost's eyes bulge out of his head, push tears out onto his cheeks. 'Buzz . . . Buzz.'

No!

We press harder. Little spit bubbles blow out the corners of Frost's mouth.

'They're going . . .'

Don't listen.

'They're going to take you away.'

You bastard!

——

——

Our head starts to hoot, we feel sick and dizzy.

Everything is black. All we can hear is Frost gargling and the thud of his blood under our thumbs.

—

—

Tom.

—

Tom!

I told you not to listen.

. . . I think we should let go.

Why?

Because he's turning purple.

We step away and Frost falls to the ground. Our head thuds. Sweat trickles down our back. We can't stop our hands from shaking, we hold them together but all that does is make our body shake as well.

What does he mean?

I don't know.

We can't breathe or think. The room spins around us. We walk over to our bed and hope it will slow down. We see our names and the date and think of all the bad things that have happened and how we don't want them to happen any more.

We need the escape plan.

'Uh-oh! Houston, we have a problem. Houston, we have a problem.'

We turn around, see Frost talking into his hand.

Have we got a plan?

Yes.

'Let me guess . . . let me guess . . . no . . . it couldn't be . . . not the beach, it couldn't be the beach. Ha!'

Is he right?

——

'Don't forget your armbands.'

Is he right?

I can't tell you. You'll tell everyone.

I won't. I can keep a secret.

You're making our head ache.

——

——

But I can keep a secret.

OK. What was the combination to Mrs Drummond's fridge?

2011.

Told you.

!

——

Are we escaping now?

We nod at Frost.

Later.

You won't go without me?

No.

Can I draw something while we're waiting?

OK.

We reach up and scratch the wall again. We imagine scraping through to the bricks, sliding them out one by one and stacking them like Lego under our bed.

And we imagine James Lewis doing the same on the other side.

—

—

Have we finished?

Yes.

We check across at Frost; his bald head is so shiny that we can't tell if he's looking at us or facing the wall. He starts to snore.

We slide off our bed, take off the sheets and blankets and rip them into strips. Then we twist them and join them together to make ropes. We need them to hang out the window.

We need them to tie up Frost.

Shush, don't tell everyone.

You started it . . . How do you tie knots again?

Like this.

?

Over, under, around the loop.

Over . . . under . . . through the loop.

Around.

Oh.

Then pull.

Like this?

Yes.

It's easy . . . Are we ready now?

No, but we've got all night.

It's cold without our sheets.

And it's cold without our blankets.
It won't be for long.

—

Can we put another jumper on?
No . . . but you can cut off one of our sleeves.
Are we making a tank top?
No, a balaclava.
Oh, like robbers?
Yes.
But I haven't got a knife.
Me neither.
I'll ask Frost—
Don't.

We pick up a jumper and rip at a hole where the arm joins the body. We bite more holes – two for our eyes, one for our mouth – and put it over our head.

I can't see. I can't see.
Turn it round.
Oh.
Ha!
Ha!
Shush!

Frost grunts and rolls over in his bed. We stand up in the middle of the room. Our heart thuds so hard it feels like we are shaking the boards. We walk towards the window.

Ready?
Yes.

Chapter Four

The moon slides out from behind the clouds and turns them silver. We put our suitcase on the ground and stand in the shadow of the wall that stretches high above us, brick on brick until it reaches the wire. We couldn't reach the top even if we stood on our shoulders.

We wish we were taller.

Shush!

We wish we were giants . . . It would be a small jump for a giant.

We put our hand over our mouth and kneel down in the shadow of the wall. We need to be quiet, we don't want to wake the dogs, we don't want to wake Mrs Unster.

A small jump for a giant—

One small step for man, one giant leap for mankind.

That's it.

We look back at the house – the TV flickers in Mrs Unster's room like she's switching channels. All the other windows are black. Everyone else is asleep inside.

Ready?

Yes.

We slide our bag off our back, swing it over the wall and hope our book won't fall apart when it lands on the other side. Our suitcase is next. We spin around like we are throwing a discus and let go. It flies through the air, bounces off the wire and comes back to us like a boomerang.

We need more velocity.

?

Speed.

We try again, and again, until our arms ache so much that we can't lift the case above our head. We put it on the ground. The catches are broken, the corners have dents, and our rockets and planes are mangled together inside.

We hear footsteps and a dog barking. We wait for a light to sweep across the grass and pin us to the wall like in *The Great Escape*.

Is this a great escape?

Not yet.

The footsteps get closer. We hear people shout.

We rummage through our suitcase. We can't take them all, we can only take our favourites, but it's hard to tell them apart in the dark. We feel under the wings, find the smooth lumps of the bombs and the sharp points of the guns – our Spitfire, our Sea Otter and our Messerschmitt Bf 109. We throw them over the wall and listen to them scrape the wires.

Where's my Lancaster?

I don't know.

But—

The footsteps get closer as the voices get louder.

We find Soyuz 8 and Apollo 9.

The dogs bark.

Where's Soyuz 11?

Where's my Lancaster?

Soyuz 11 is more important.

Because it's yours?

Because it's the rocket that took Dad to the moon.

We find it in the corner under our jumper with the other rockets. We throw them over the wall and hope their parachutes will open before they hit the ground. We lean our suitcase against the wall, climb on top and scramble up like a spider. The wire tugs at our shirt and snags on our trousers.

'You no escape.'

We look back. Mrs Unster stands below us, shining a torch in our eyes.

'You never escape.' She walks towards us, gets so close that we think she can reach up and grab us.

We wriggle on the wire, but the more we do, the deeper it cuts.

It hurts.

I know.

We stop wriggling and remember what Dad told us.

One small step—

At the airfield!

. . . Never talk when—

Play dead.

—

—

We lie still on the wire. The torch makes purple spots in our eyes.

Don't blink.

I won't.

We hear the sound of metal scraping as a man runs, dragging a ladder across the ground.

I think we should—

Not yet.

'Ha!' Mrs Unster bends down and picks up a plane. 'I see you bomb Berlin no more.' She lifts up our Lancaster and lets it crash to the ground.

!

I'll get you another.

When?

When we've escaped.

When will that be?

The man leans the ladder against the wall.

When will that be?

When the enemy least expects it.

When's that?

Now!

We twist our body and roll. The wire digs further into our knee, our trousers rip, our leg breaks free and we are left kneeling on top of the wall.

Engage launch control. Engage launch control.

?

Jump!

Oh.

We fly through the air and land next to our bag on the other side. Our Sea Otter and our rockets are by the wall, the fighters are by the first trees in the wood.

Crank engines!

No, not now.

We hold the fighters above our heads.

Turn propellers.

Jack, just run.

Can we go back for my Lancaster?

No.

Because of Mrs Unster?

Because it'll slow us down.

?

We'd have to dump fuel in the Channel and drop the bombs on France.

. . . And we don't want to bomb France?

No.

. . . Because you like cheese?

You're wasting our breath.

We hold the planes up high, see their wings tilt left and right as they cut across the moon and we run

88

between tall trees with our book in our bag. The Messerschmitt climbs high. The Spitfire climbs higher. We increase the throttle and disappear into the dark.

Jack and Tom Gagarin were here

1973–1976

But now they are gone

Chapter Five

We are running. We are running scared. Our legs are aching, our lungs are burning. We want to stop but we have to keep going.

We run through the woods following the light of our torch. The trees look like shadows and the shadows look like people. We dodge between them. Our shoulders scrape on the bark, our balaclava on the branches. We try to untangle it but our fingers are shaking.

We have to keep going.

Because the shadows are coming.

And the dogs are snarling.

We leave our balaclava hanging like a pumpkin from a tree.

We reach a stream that runs fast and cold. The water rushes around our feet and our feet stumble over stones. The further we go, the deeper it gets. We put our torch in our mouth and hold our bag over our head.

We can't speak.

We can't breathe.

Our body is frozen when we reach the other side.

We stop at a hut at the edge of the woods and hide from car lights that flash down the road. Our bag is heavy.

Our trainers are squelching.

We wring out our shirt and trousers and put them back on.

We wish we had a blanket.

We wish we were in bed.

In the home?

In our house.

Our real house?

Yes, when we were safe and warm.

We wish we could ride our bikes to the shop.

We wish we could stay up late with Mum and Dad on a Saturday night and spend Sunday morning in bed.

We wish—

Shush!

We hear a snapping sound.

Like crocodiles biting.

Like branches snapping.

We pour the water out of our trainers, cross the road and run back into the woods.

We imagine we are like Dad when he was in the army, crawling on the ground, hiding behind trees with our gun on our back and a grenade in our hand. We stop, listen for dogs.

Can we shoot?

—

Can we throw the grenade?

I said we imagine.

We throw a grenade into the air.

Boom!

We run on until our legs get heavy and our head gets dizzy. We stumble, fall over and can't get back up.

Can we stay here?

—

Can we?

We roll over. Dead leaves rustle around our ears, dead branches snap under our back.

OK.

We rest our head on our bag. It's not as comfortable as our pillow but at least we are free from the walls we have left behind. Now the sky is our ceiling and the ground is our bed. We lie and listen to the darkness, our heartbeat on the earth, the wind through the woods. We know we should keep going but we ache too much to move. We know we should read but it's too dark to see the words. But after three years of reading we can remember them all.

Summer 1971

The church was dark and cold the day I went to bury Jack. I stood at the front watching the vicar. He was standing with his arms against his chest and a Bible in his hands. People were coughing and whispering behind me but every time I turned around to see who it was, the coughing and whispering stopped. At the back, by the door, two firemen were talking to two friends of Dad's from the army, Tony and Geoff. Tony waved when he saw me looking, Geoff touched the peak of his cap. It was the first time I'd seen them since Dad had gone to the moon. I thought of waving back but then the big doors opened and four men in black coats carried Jack's coffin in. I couldn't stop staring at it as it came down the aisle towards me. It was like the coffin was the only thing that was moving in the whole world. I thought of Jack inside, how much he would hate being trapped in the dark. I thought of him running around on the grass, holding his planes over his head, jumping over paths. And I imagined myself running with him and wished we could do it again.

My eyes bulged with tears. Auntie Jean put her arm around me and gave me a tissue.

I hadn't seen Jack since the day after he died. He was gone when I woke up in the morning. There was no lump beside me, no pile of clothes at the end of the bed. For three days I went looking for him in the places we used to play: up on our hill, outside the shop, in the park. People seemed to be watching me wherever I went. Some stared as they walked by, some smiled and some stopped and talked. But I couldn't hear what they were saying and I couldn't reply. I just stared back at them while cars and buses went by with no rumble of engines or exhaust; it was like they were silently floating on air. I kept on looking for Jack, in the chip shop, on the road to town. I even checked at his school but he wasn't there either.

I listened to the shuffle of the men's feet as the coffin got closer. My legs started to shake, my head went dizzy. Auntie Jean squeezed my hand and I screwed up my eyes tight. I heard the vicar speak, people coughed, a baby cried. I screwed up my eyes tighter, tried to imagine Jack pushing up the lid, jumping out, then running up and down the aisle. And I imagined myself following him, circling the altar, climbing over the pews, running for the door.

It was raining when I got outside. I pulled my hood up and walked between the tombstones that stuck up out of the dead grass. Some of them had little vases of flowers on them, some of them had pebbles or little pieces of slate, and some of them were surrounded by weeds. The further I walked, the louder the rain sounded on my hood and the more it dripped off the edges down onto my nose.

I looked further up the hill. Auntie Jean was at the top being blown around with her purple umbrella. She had asked me if I wanted her to walk with me. I told her I was OK, I wanted one last chance to look for Jack, but the further I walked, the more I thought he wouldn't come back. I passed one of the men in black coats, resting against one of the cars. He smiled at me and nodded further up the hill. I walked on, past more grave-stones, and stopped when I reached Auntie Jean standing by a pile of earth.

There were another two men wearing black coats, an old man with a spade and the vicar was there sniffing and blowing his nose. He looked at me and smiled, then took one step towards Jack's grave. He nodded at me to do the same then pulled a red Bible from his sleeve.

'Friends and family, we are gathered here ...' The rain sounded louder on my hood, I pulled it back behind my ears. The vicar kept reading. 'We thank the Lord for Jack, he has gone, but we shouldn't feel sad; sometimes God reaches out and takes little people early.'

I shivered as the wind blew through the trees and blew the pages of the Bible. The vicar screwed up his nose, marked his place with his finger, then lifted his head back and sneezed.

'Bless me,' he said. 'Sorry ... where were we?'

'We were being grateful,' I said.

He smiled down at me. 'Ah, yes ... We should be grateful for the time that Jack spent with us on Earth, for his little trips to the beach ... and the park, and of course for all the times he climbed the hill with his brother, Tom.'

He smiled again. But I couldn't smile back. I couldn't help thinking that if he thought Jack's life was so great, then God could have let him enjoy it a little longer. He'd only just reached double figures.

'It's not bloody fair!' I shouted.

The two men in black coats looked at each other.

The old man fell off his spade.

I took two steps forward. The vicar grabbed my arm.

'Don't jump,' he said.

The wind brushed over the top of my head, whistled around my ears and rustled through the trees. I crouched down, put my hands over my head. God had already reached out for Jack. I hoped he hadn't come back for me.

'Tom, what are you doing?'

I looked up, across the hole in the earth, wiped the tears and rain out of my eyes.

'Jack?'

'That's me.'

Jack was sitting on his coffin on the far side of the hole. He smiled. I felt sweat run down my back under my shirt.

'I thought . . . I thought you'd gone.'

He started to giggle as he pointed at my trousers.

'What are you wearing?'

I looked down. The pins that Auntie Jean had stuck in my trousers were glistening in the rain. I pulled them up until the belt touched my ribs.

'Auntie Jean gave them to me,' I said. 'They belonged to Eric.'

Jack laughed.

Auntie Jean put her hand on my shoulder.

'Tom,' she said, 'aren't you feeling well?'

I didn't answer because Jack's laugh got louder and then suddenly stopped.

'Why aren't you laughing?' he asked.

I nodded at Auntie Jean and then the vicar.

'Because people don't laugh at funerals.'

Jack put his hand over his mouth.

'Ooops. Sorry . . . Are you burying your friend?'

'Kind of.'

'So you're not burying him?'

'Yes.'

'But it's not your friend?'

'Well . . .' I glanced at his coffin.

Jack turned his head sideways and started to read the name written on the brass plate.

'Jack . . . Jack Gag . . . Me?'

I nodded.

Jack screwed up his face and I watched as his eyes turned from blue to black in the rain.

I wanted to jump over the hole and give him a hug but the two men in black coats walked over and picked up the ends of the ropes. The coffin rocked. Jack wobbled on top.

'Am I getting buried in this?'

I nodded.

'But it's not very big.'

'Neither are you.'

'But I might grow.'

'I don't think you will.'

Auntie Jean bent down, water streamed off her umbrella into the hole.

'Tom,' she said, 'what are you doing?'

My teeth were chattering, the rain was dripping off my chin. I held out my hand, Jack held out his and we reached for each other across the hole. My knees sunk into the mud but I stretched out further and our hands met in the middle. He smiled. I wanted to hold his hand tight and never let go, but it was soft, wet and black like newspaper. A finger broke off. Jack slipped away from me and I started to cry.

The vicar bent down.

'Young man,' he said, 'did you want a little longer to say goodbye?'

I didn't answer. I looked down into the hole, tried to see Jack's finger, but all I could see was the soil. I looked over at Jack. He was kneeling up, sniffing the fingers he had left.

'Tom, how did I die?'

I shrugged. I'd had four days to come up with an answer. If I'd known he was going to come back again I would have thought harder. I looked up at the vicar. I looked over at the two men with the ropes. I looked across at the man with the shovel. They were all staring at me. I tried to swallow. Jack looked up at the sky.

'Did it work, Tom? Did we find Dad?'

'What's he saying?' asked the vicar.

'I don't know,' said Auntie Jean.

'No, Jack, it didn't work.'

'Was it my fault?'

'No, not really,' I said.

'Will you tell me later?'

'Yes.'

'After I'm buried?'

I nodded.

The vicar coughed, then he blessed the earth, and blessed the heavens, and he blessed himself when he sneezed again.

The rain stopped and the sun came out. Jack walked round the hole and stood next to me. The man walked over from the car and picked up one of the ropes on the other side. One end of a rope lay spare on the ground.

'Is that one for you?' Jack asked.

'I don't know.'

'Did you carry my coffin?'

'No. I was too short to go on the corner.'

Jack pushed his eyebrows together.

'You would have tipped out.'

'Oh.'

I looked at the rope. It was too heavy for my arms, too thick for my hands. I looked around for help but no one else looked like they were going to pick up the rope. I heard a horn blast, then the rumble of traffic. I looked up the hill, over the gravestones that stretched on and on until they stopped at a wall by the road. A double-decker bus went by with its windows steamed up and silhouettes of people sitting inside. I looked ahead of it, towards the gates. A tall man with dark hair walked in circles between them, looking at the ground. He lifted his head, ran his hand through his hair and looked over at me.

'Dad?'

'Where?' Jack jumped up.

I pointed to the gates.

'I can't see him.'

The vicar bent down.

'Is there something wrong?'

'It's our dad,' I said.

'It's our dad,' said Jack.

The vicar shrugged at Auntie Jean. Auntie Jean shrugged back then looked at me.

'I don't think so, my love,' she said.

The man just stood and stared.

He was thinner than Dad. Dad was big, he used to play rugby for the army, but he would have lost weight after eating space food all summer. I looked around the cemetery to see where his rocket could have landed. I looked back at the gate, but in the time I had turned away the man had disappeared into the exhaust fumes from the bus.

'Was it him, Tom?'

'No.'

'How do you know?'

'He wasn't wearing his spacesuit.'

—

The man with the spade picked up the fourth rope. The ropes went taut as the coffin slid across the grass, hovered over the hole and slowly moved out of the sunlight into the dark. Jack squirmed beside me and made a noise like a cat trying to meow with its mouth closed.

'Am I going to heaven, Tom?'

'I hope so.'

'But isn't heaven up there?' He pointed between the trees to the sky.

—

'Tom?'

'What?'

'I think I'm going the wrong way.'

The coffin rested on the bottom. The sun went behind a cloud. I held out my hand and looked down, but Jack was gone.

I shivered. The rain had soaked through my coat to Eric's suit and Eric's suit was stuck to my skin. The vicar bent down and asked me if I was OK. I told him I was cold.

'Me too.'

I looked in the hole, down the hill, up at the sky. I couldn't see Jack, but I could still hear his voice.

'Jack. Where are you?'

'Here?'

'Where's that?'

'Here.'

I felt a buzz inside my head, like a wasp flying around in a can. It got quicker and quicker, louder and louder, until it reached the middle. I put my hands over my ears and tried to shake Jack loose, but the buzzing just got louder and my head started to vibrate. I screwed up my eyes. I heard Jack laughing then suddenly he stopped as the men slid another coffin out of a car and carried it across to the grave.

'Tom, what's happening? Did I split into two parts?'

The vicar coughed, put one hand on my shoulder. I didn't know if it was to help me or to stop him from falling over.

'Friends and family. We are gathered here . . .'

'He already said this bit.'

'I know. Jack . . . there's something I've been meaning to tell you.'

'Our plan didn't work?'

'No. It's—'

The vicar bent down. I smelt strawberry medicine on his breath. 'We can stop for a while if you like,' he said.

'I'm OK.'

'I'm not.'

'It's OK,' he said. 'You're bound to be confused.' He stood back up and started to read the Bible.

'I am the resurrection and the life, saith the Lord; he that believeth in me, though he were dead . . .'

'What happened?'

'I know that my Redeemer liveth, and that He shall stand at the latter day . . .'

'Did the spies get through the radar?'

'Jack,' I said. 'I think we should be listening.'

'It's boring.'

The vicar's voice grew louder.

'Blessed are the dead who die in the Lord . . .'

'Is it important?'

'I think this bit is.'

'Into Thy hands, O merciful Saviour, we commend Thy servant, Miriam.'

'Miriam?'

'From dust were you made, O man, and to dust shall you return . . .'

'Jack, I'm sorry, I tried to tell you.'

The men picked up the ropes and lifted the coffin over the hole. I leant over and stared down at Jack's coffin in the dark as the men let out the ropes and slowly lowered Mum in on top.

The funeral cars seemed to slide down the hill and all I could hear was the sound of tyres picking up stones. I walked towards the gates with Auntie Jean tap-tap-tapping beside me, using her umbrella as a walking stick. She talked all the way down, only stopping three times to catch her breath. She told me that she knew what it felt like to be alone, that sometimes, during the day, or in the middle of the night, she would talk to her Eric. She said it helped her to think that he was listening. I kept walking, looking at the ground, scuffing stones. Auntie Jean followed. I knew she was only trying to make me feel better, but what she did with Eric was different – her Eric just listened, he didn't keep talking inside her head.

There was a taxi waiting when we reached the gates. Auntie Jean opened the door, I climbed in and she sat beside me in the back. The seats smelt of beer and cigarettes. I wound down the window and put my head out as we went down the hill, past the park, into town.

We stopped at roadworks by the hospital. The smell of tarmac drifted out of a barrel and made me choke. I looked up at the building. The sun was reflecting in the windows with clouds rushing from the top to the bottom like the world had slipped onto its side. I searched for the room Mum used to be in, top row, three in from the end, the one with the dull orange light that turned everyone into shadows. I thought of her lying in her bed, covered in bandages with two slits cut away for her eyes, two more for her mouth and nose, and two tubes coming out of her and going into a machine.

A yellow digger passed by. My head rumbled against the glass, but I couldn't hear its engine, all I could hear was the hiss, click, clunk of Mum breathing into the machine – twelve times a minute, 720 times an hour, 17,280 times a day. I tried to remember holding her hand, it was smooth and warm, but it didn't move – hiss, click, clunk. Hiss, click, clunk—

I'd sat in a chair by her side. She wasn't very big when she was stood up, she looked even smaller when she was lying down. I looked at her face, it wasn't smooth and white like I remembered it. She had a wrinkled red mark that ran like a zip from her eye down to her neck. And her hair had gone frizzy, turned from blonde to brown like it did when she came back from town after getting caught in the rain – hiss, click, clunk. Hiss, click, clunk – the doctors and nurses circled at the end of her bed and whispered in the dark. They said something about three days, something about burns and something about more drugs. I didn't know what any of it meant, but from the way they shook their heads I knew they didn't think Mum was going to get better.

I told them they were wrong, that if they'd sat with Mum for as long as I had they would have seen her jerk her hand ten times a day and blink five times every hour. And she was getting better, she was breathing into the machine. I remember a doctor crouching down and rubbing my head. I remember him smiling and touching my arm, I remember my body went empty when he spoke.

'Tom, your mum's not breathing into the machine, the machine is breathing into her.'

The lights turned green and the taxi drove on. My eyes began to water in the wind. I saw the taxi driver watching me in his wing mirror. I wiped my tears on my arm. I think he smiled.

We followed the river out of town. Sometimes it disappeared behind buildings, the milk depot and the petrol station, and sometimes we had to go around roundabouts, but it wasn't long before the road met up with the river again. I remembered Dad walking this way to town. I thought of all the hot days that I had watched him from our hill and all the hot nights that me and Jack had spent waiting for him to come home. If he hadn't gone to the moon none of this would have happened. He would still be here, Mum would still be here and Jack would be sitting next to me in his Chelsea kit kicking the front seat and not running around inside my head.

I thought about all the times we went to hospital when Jack was little, when he woke up not being able to breathe in the middle of the night. I remembered his chest going up and down. I remembered him gulping air and I remembered him laughing at me as he ate hospital jelly in an oxygen tent. And I thought how much I wished he was sitting beside me. Now I was the only Gagarin left.

I turned and looked at Auntie Jean; she was asleep with her head back on the seat. Her mouth was wide open like she was eating an apple. She started to snore. I thought about what it would be like to live with her. She wouldn't be able to take me to football, and, at weekends, I could only listen to it on the radio. It wouldn't be as exciting as watching it on TV.

The taxi's indicators clicked as it turned into our road. Everything was quiet as we drove past the houses, all their curtains were drawn, all their windows were shut and as we got closer to my house I closed my eyes and smelt the smoke again.

Four days after the funeral Auntie Jean said she was tired. I heard her talking while I was walking around amongst the pieces of melted plastic and twisted metal in our back garden. It was early, the sky was full of birds. I crept over to the fence.

'I'm so tired,' Auntie Jean said. 'I just can't sleep.'

I peered through a gap in the fence and saw Auntie Jean talking to a rose bush on the other side. There was a whisper but the words got mixed up with the sound of the radio from the kitchen. She cupped her hand around her ear and leant forward.

'What's that?'

I heard a snipping sound. Mrs French stood up on the other side of the bush with a pair of scissors in her hand. She puffed out her cheeks and wiped sweat off her brow.

'It's this damned heat, I can't sleep either.'

Auntie Jean shook her head.

'No,' she said. 'It's the boy . . .'

'Oh . . . Poor lad. It's terrible for those left behind.'

I pressed my eye against the fence. Auntie Jean nodded.

'I know . . . I know.'

Mrs French lifted her scissors and cut a head off a rose.

'Will he be staying with you?'

'No, he can't stay . . . He doesn't stop talking.'

Mrs French smiled. 'Well, it's good he can talk to you.'

'No . . .' Auntie Jean put her hand up to the side of her mouth. 'To himself,' she said, 'to his brother . . . I heard him through the wall.'

Mrs French dropped her scissors. Auntie Jean walked down the garden, squeezed through a gap between the bushes and joined Mrs French on the other side. Music played on the radio. I saw their mouths move but I couldn't hear what they were saying.

A gust of wind whistled around me, blew pieces of burnt paper up into the air. Puffs of black ash blew from our window-sills. I slid down the fence, closed my eyes and wrapped my hands around my head. The wind blew harder, I peeped through my fingers. The ash mixed with the paper turned the sky grey and blocked out the sun.

'Is she sending us away?' Jack asked.

'I think so.'

'What about if Dad comes back? How will he find us?'

'I don't know.'

'How do we tell him we moved? How will the postman know where to deliver his letters?'

I told him to be quiet, that I was trying to listen, but he kept repeating the same thing over and over again.

'What about Dad? What about Dad?'

I squeezed my head tighter.

'I don't know,' I shouted. 'Jack, I don't know.'

There was a bang, the fence shook behind me. I looked up and saw Auntie Jean rushing down our garden path towards me. I put my head on my knees.

'It's OK,' she said. 'You'll be OK.' She crouched down by my side.

'Will I?'

She nodded.

'And Jack?'

'What's that?'

'And Jack?'

She put her arm around me and took me back inside. I didn't hear her reply.

I stayed in for the rest of the day. Auntie Jean said she was tired, that she'd just listen to her radio, maybe do some knitting. I sat on the settee, sometimes looking out of the window, sometimes watching the clock on the mantelpiece. For a second I thought of going outside and playing football, but I couldn't take a penalty and be in goal at the same time. And all the time I was thinking Jack was there chattering away inside my head.

I looked at the clock again; only five minutes had passed. I looked at Auntie Jean, saw her looking at me. We did that all afternoon, looked at each other without talking, then she'd smile, check her watch and look out the window like she was waiting for a bus. I didn't want to leave our house behind but I knew I couldn't stay with her, I couldn't sit with her in silence because it just made the voice in my head even worse. It was great to have Jack back but there was no escape, I couldn't turn him on and off like a TV. A lump grew in my throat. I stared out the window and thought about a time when me and Jack were with Mum and Dad and we were all happy.

Dad had taken the day off work and we'd had a picnic out on the lawn. Mum was lying on her back with her hair spread on the grass as she tried to catch the sun. Dad made rabbit shadows with his hands, made them jump across her body. Me and Jack started to giggle. Dad put his finger up to his lips. Then he made another rabbit jump from Mum's feet and nibble her ear. I put my hand over my mouth. Jack laughed out loud. Mum opened her eyes, squinted at the sun.

'What are you up to?' she asked.

Dad stood up straight, put his hands by his side like he was on parade.

'Nothing,' he said.

'Are you sure, Corporal?' said Mum.

Dad looked at me and Jack without turning his head. His eyes started to water, a smirk grew across his face and turned into a grin. He lifted up his hand and pointed at me and Jack.

'It was them,' he said.

'It was you,' I said.

'It was you,' said Jack.

Dad laughed, stamped his foot on the ground. Me and Jack

got up and he chased us as we ran around in circles. Mum took off her shoes and joined in. It was Dad chasing me and Jack, and Mum chasing him. Our circles got faster and bigger. I heard Mum giggle, I could hear Dad laugh as he reached out with his hand and tried to grab the tail of my shirt. I shouted to Jack.

'He's catching us,' I said.

Jack's eyes were wide open like a mouse's. We broke out of the circle, ran across our lawn and onto Auntie Jean's. We jumped the path onto Mr Green's and Mum and Dad followed. I could still hear him shouting, hear him laughing, he was getting so close I could feel his breath on my neck. Jack started to slow.

'Got you!'

Jack screamed and curled up in a ball on the grass. I ran on.

'I'm still here, still going to catch you.' Dad tugged on my shirt again. I tried to run faster but Dad's laugh made me laugh, made my breath run out, turned my legs to jelly. I started to fall. He grabbed me, wrapped me in his arms and we fell to the ground together. He started to tickle me, then stopped as Mum and Jack caught up with us and fell on top.

I rested my head against the window and wished we could all be together now.

A snoring sound made me jump.

I turned around. Auntie Jean had fallen asleep on the settee. I left her there sleeping and went upstairs. The bedroom door was ajar. My suitcase was lying open on the bed and my shoes were in a plastic bag on top. Jack asked where we were going. I told him I didn't know but wherever we were going it looked like we would be leaving soon. I packed the rockets. Jack helped me pack the planes.

It was while we were flying the Spitfire that I heard the front door click open, then slam. I went to the window and watched Auntie Jean shuffle up the garden path, then cut across the bottom of our hill. For somebody who was tired she was moving very fast.

She knocked on Mrs Green's door and went into her hallway. I waited five minutes until I saw her again in Mrs Green's sitting room looking out the window at me.

Mrs Green drank tea.

Auntie Jean just stared.

Mrs Green ate biscuits.

Auntie Jean ate her fingers.

I could see that she was right, she really was tired. While I had one person in my head, she had two of us talking in her house. But I didn't think she was physically tired, I think she was just tired of being our auntie. If she had given me and Jack a chance she might have got used to it. She liked Jack when he was alive, he hadn't changed much now that he was dead. He still wanted to play with his Action Man, he still wanted to run to the shops, the only difference was that when we bought gobstoppers we had to cram them all in my mouth because they couldn't go in his.

But Auntie Jean had got jumpy. On the last evening I stayed with her she couldn't stop her newspaper from shaking. I asked her what was wrong.

'It's nothing,' she said. 'I'm just getting old and when people get old they get colder.'

'But the weatherman said it's been the hottest summer.'

She put her paper down and smiled. But it wasn't a real smile. It was a smile where her lips moved while her eyes stared into space. I wanted a hug, something to make me feel better, but as I sat looking at her I realised that I would be gone in the morning and I would never see her again.

Chapter Six

The moon has disappeared and the sky has turned grey.
We stand in the middle of a circle with mist around our
knees, surrounded by the trees that trapped us as we
slept through the night. We can't see a gap to get out.

We can't see the tracks where we came in.

Shush!

What?

We're thinking.

Are we?

We pick up our bag and start to run. The trees get
further apart until we run out into a field. We jump
over a gate and run up a track with grass growing in
the middle until our path is blocked by a gate. We climb
over, run across a yard into a barn.

A million chickens—

?

A thousand?

A hundred chickens cluck inside.

We run through the middle. They run for cover. We
try to jump over them but every time we land they
seem to be under our feet. One flies through the air,

smashes against the barn wall and lands in a pile of straw.

Its wing flaps.

Its head hangs down.

Is it dead?

I think so.

But we didn't mean to kill it.

No.

We run out of the barn and back into the yard.

Our eyes sting in the light.

Our throat is sore.

We hear the sound of an engine. A farmer comes towards us on a tractor with smoke pouring out the back. We run out of the yard and into a field. Our legs turn to jelly as we stumble and roll down a hill – over and over – face the sky, face the dirt, face the sky, face the dirt. We stop at the bottom by a water trough. Our heart is thumping, our head is so dizzy that the cows spin on the hills around us. We put our hands on the side of the trough and pull ourself up. Blood thumps through our palms, our body is shaking. We lean over the trough, see the sun in the water and ourself reflected with our mouth wide open. Blood drips off our hand into the trough.

We're bleeding to death!

——

We put our arm in the water – what looks like a deep cut washes away to a scratch. We think about where we might have done it, that the dogs might find it and follow our scent. We can't let them catch us. We can't let them take us back.

——

We look back up the hill and listen.
Are they coming?

——

Are they coming?
I don't know.

——

We look back down, see our reflection shimmering in the water. Our mouth hangs open, our eyes are bulged wide. The clouds rush behind us. Suddenly we feel small because the world is so much bigger now we are outside.

We take our bag off our back, put it on the ground and look back up the hill. A plastic bag blows in the wind, our book is open beside it with Dad's letters scattered between the cows. We don't want to go back but we can't leave everything behind.

Because the dogs will sniff our scent?

Because people won't be able to read our story.

We walk back up the hill. Our trainers are covered in cow dung, the cow dung is covered in flies. We pick up the letters one by one, put them in our book and go back to the trough to check for damage. The corners of our book are crumpled, the picture on the front is smudged. We open it and check inside.

This book belongs to me.
This book belongs to him.
If you find it please return
it to us.

The outside might be damaged but the first words we wrote have survived. Mum was with us when we wrote them in the kitchen. She said it was nice but not grammatically correct.

?

. . . It didn't make sense.

Didn't it?

Not then.

But it does now?

Yes. Dad told us one day everything would make sense.

Even his letters?

I think so.

Can we read one now?

——

Can we read one now? Beep.

I heard, I just think we should keep going.

But Dad's letters aren't very long.

We look over our shoulder to see if anyone is chasing but the only thing that follows us are our footprints through the dung.

OK.

Good.

But only one.

OK.

We flick to the back of our book and open a letter from the moon.

17th June 1971

Dear Jack. Dear Tom.

Today I am sitting by the window in the sun but no matter how many times we spin I can't get warm.

Georgi says Brrrrrr!

Sorry about the writing. Viktor has lent me his gloves but there are no holes for my thumbs.

Viktor says Brrrrrr!

Tom, sometimes I look out the window and in the middle of the oceans I see all the islands. You would love them, they are the footsteps of giants.

I will keep searching for the giant.

Jack, I haven't seen your monster.

Got to go, Viktor wants his gloves back.

Love, Dad.

And Georgi. HA

And Viktor. HO

———

———

We read the letter again in our head and think about Dad, how it was weird that he was cold even though he was sitting in the sun.

And we think about the monsters.

———

And the giants, and their footprints around the earth . . .

A shadow swoops across the ground towards us, the light flashes as it crosses the sun. We look up and see a bird hovering in the air above us.

We think it might be a hawk.

We think it might be a spy.

———

It rises and falls before it lands on a telephone wire.

We put the letter back in the book.

———

———

Tom?

———

Tom!

What?

I think we need to keep running.

Me too.

And we need to keep reading.

I know.

Summer 1971

Dad's army uniform was hung on the banister at the bottom of the stairs. The collar was dusty and the sleeves were creased. It had two medals on the front, above the chest pocket, and three silver numbers on the shoulder. 606. That was Dad's army number. He told us once that it was a palindrome, that it would come in handy if ever he had to march backwards.

What's a palindrome?
It's a word or a number that reads the same whichever way you look at it.
Like Exeter?
?
Like Exeter?
No, that's just got lots of 'e's in it.
Oh.

It was Dad's birthday. Me and Jack were sitting on the bottom stair waiting for him. We'd been there for an hour but in the week since he'd started his new job it was getting later and later before Dad came home. We didn't know what he was doing, he seemed too busy to tell us. I thought he was a postman.

Jack thought he was a milkman. They were the only jobs we could think of where you had to get up earlier than the sun.

I climbed up two stairs and looked into the sitting room. Mum was sitting on the settee with the cake she'd made for Dad on the table. I put my head between the spindles of the banister.

'How much longer?'

Mum checked her watch with the clock on the mantelpiece and turned around.

'I don't know, Tom.' She looked down at the cake and the card that me and Jack had made. 'I don't know, but it shouldn't be long now.'

I bumped back down the stairs and sat next to Jack.

'I don't think Mum knows what his job is either,' I whispered.

Jack shrugged, rested his head against Dad's jacket. I leant against the wall and we sat in silence and stared at the door. I thought maybe if we watched it long enough it might make Dad come home quicker, like when we waited for a bus with Mum. My feet got cold, Jack got fed up and went in and joined Mum watching TV in the sitting room. I looked at the door; the glass at the top was beginning to turn dark and Dad still hadn't come home.

Jack was asleep on the settee when Dad's key finally turned in the lock. I put my hand on his legs and shook him awake while Mum turned the sound down on the TV. My heart started to beat faster as the cold night air came through the hall. Dad

closed the door. I waited for him to shout 'Anybody in? . . .
Everybody out?' like he always did, but all I heard was a shuffle
and a rustle as he slipped off his shoes and put his coat on the
hook.

Jack picked up our card. I picked up the matches and went
to strike one but stopped as Mum put her hand on top of
mine. She shook her head.

I turned and saw Dad standing in the doorway. His head
used to nearly touch the top, now it was rested on the side
like he was going to go asleep against the frame.

'Are you all right, Steve?' Mum asked.

Dad looked at the cake and muttered something, it sounded
like he was talking backwards. Then he shook his head slowly
and walked back into the hall. I put the matches down on the
table. Mum told us to stay still as she got up off the settee and
followed Dad out into the hall. I wanted to find out what was
wrong but when I heard them whispering in the kitchen I could
tell they were talking about something they didn't want us to
hear.

I lay back with Jack on the settee. We couldn't listen but
we couldn't think of anything to say either. We sat together
and watched the TV screen flicker. I remember seeing the
start of *Panorama*. I remember thinking I wanted to go to
sleep.

Mum made me jump when she came back in and sat down
beside me. She said Dad had gone to bed, that he was sorry
he'd not opened his card and that he'd open it in the morning.

She yawned and her eyes started to water. I tapped Jack on the leg, told him it was time for bed, but he just made a grunting sound and rolled over. Mum put her hand on my knee.

'Tom,' she said, 'what do you want to be when you grow up?' Her voice was soft and slow like she was too tired to talk. I wondered why she was asking. I thought maybe someone had called from school, that Mr Giles had told her I hadn't done my RE homework or I'd been late back from break.

'Have I done something wrong?' I asked.

Mum smiled. 'No, I'm just asking.' She rubbed my knee. I felt the warmth of her hand go through my pyjamas.

'But you know,' I said. 'You know I want to be a writer.'

'That's what I thought,' she said. She leant forward and reached under the settee. I watched as she slid out a plastic bag and put it on the table.

'It's for you,' she said.

I opened the bag. Inside was a book, it was bigger than my exercise books at school but smaller than my encyclopaedia. I took it out and flicked through the pages.

'There's nothing in it,' I said.

Mum smiled. 'You're the writer,' she said.

'But what do I write about?'

'Everything. Just write about the things you do every day.'

'At school?'

'Yes.'

'And with Jack . . . and Dad?'

She nodded. 'Everyone,' she said.

Jack wriggled beside me. I flicked through the book again; there were hundreds of pages. I wondered how I could write enough words to fill them and how, even if I could, I didn't think enough would happen in my life for people to read it. I saw Mum looking at me.

'It's OK,' she said. 'You've got all summer.'

Jack sat up. 'Can I help?'

I looked at him. He shrugged. I thought he'd been asleep but he'd been listening all the time. 'I could draw pictures,' he said.

'You can do it together,' Mum said. 'You can write what you like as long as it's true.'

'Like the Bible,' I said.

'Yes, like the Bible, and you two can be my disciples.'

I wanted to get up early the next morning to give Dad his card but I only woke up when I heard the front door slam. I thought of just letting Dad go and giving him his card when he got home, but as I lay on my bed staring at the ceiling I remembered what Mum had said to us the night before. I sat up on my bed and saw my book on the table beside me. Now I had a book to write I had to follow Dad wherever he went.

I ran to the landing window and looked out. The sky was empty. Without the moon or the sun I couldn't tell if it was blue or grey. I looked down at the ground. Dad was already walking down the path past the electricity substation at the end of Auntie Jean's garden. I turned to go and get Jack but he was already by my side putting his slippers on. I put mine on and we ran down the stairs, out onto the path and into the back lane. Dad had reached the bottom, gone past the wire fence of the football ground, and was turning a corner at the end. We ran after him as fast as we could, jumping behind lamp posts, hiding between cars. We watched Dad like detectives, with imaginary cigarettes between our fingers and smoke puffing from our mouths.

When Dad reached the chip shop he started to run. I started to run again but the faster I ran, the further away Dad got. I heard a shout and turned round. Jack was bent over trying to breathe. Dad had got too fast for us since he'd swapped his uniform and boots for his red tracksuit and trainers. I ran back to Jack.

'I'm sorry,' he said. He started to cough and his eyes filled with water. 'Have we lost him?'

I put my hand on his back. 'It's OK,' I said. 'We'll watch him from the hill.'

We walked back home. Jack got his inhaler, I got my binoculars and together we walked up the hill.

We stopped halfway up and I took my binoculars out of their case. Jack told me to hurry. I told him I had to be careful. I flicked off the dust covers and cleaned the lenses like Dad had shown me, then held them up to my eyes.

I scanned across the rooftops, down towards the river and on to the main road as it headed into town. I saw a man walking with a briefcase, an old lady with two dogs and the milkman putting the bottles back in his van. I scanned ahead, past the milk yard and the petrol station. I found Dad running along the pavement just before it ran out under the railway arch.

He disappeared into the dark. My binoculars went blurred, my head went dizzy as I searched ahead and waited for him to come out the other side. Jack tugged my arm, said he wanted to look. I pulled the lenses wide apart so that we could share and we watched as Dad ran out of the tunnel, past the petrol station and started to slow down by the park. He stopped and checked his watch.

'What's he doing?' Jack whispered.

Our heads bumped together.

'I think he's waiting for the bus.'

We looked back along the road, saw a red one travelling towards him. But when we looked back for Dad he was already off and running, cutting his way through the park, getting smaller and smaller until he was just a little red speck weaving in and out of the shadows of the trees.

My arm started to ache. Jack took the binoculars and pushed them back together to fit his eyes.

'I can see him,' he shouted. 'I can see him . . . but . . .'

'But what?'

'But now he's gone.'

'Where?'

Jack took the binoculars down. He had a look on his face like he was stuck with his maths. He lifted up his arm and pointed.

'In there,' he said.

I put my head by the side of his and followed the line of his finger as he pointed to the tall building with big glass windows on the other side of the valley. We looked at each other. We'd never seen Dad go there before.

I was painting a Hawker when Dad came home at the end of the day. Jack was on the floor watching TV and playing with his Lego. Dad sat beside me on the settee. His face was white, he had black rings around his eyes and his hair was standing on end. He pointed at my plane, told me I'd missed a bit between the bombs and the fuselage, but I didn't really care, I just wanted to know where he'd been all day.

He lay back against a cushion and yawned. I saw water glisten in his eyes. He held out his arm and I lay back against his body. He smelt different, like he'd swapped his aftershave for disinfectant. I sniffed. Dad looked down at me and frowned like he was stuck on a crossword.

'Got a cold, Tom?' he asked.

'No,' I said. 'It's just that you smell different.'

Dad laughed, lifted up his arm and sniffed the back of his hand.

'It's just soap, Tom,' he said, 'where I washed them at work.'

I put my head back on his chest. I smelt the soap again. It wasn't just on his hands, it was all over his body. I went to speak again but stopped as Dad put his arm back around me and I felt him rest his head on mine. I felt it get heavier and heavier.

Jack stood up and picked a piece of paper off the table.

'I've drawn you a picture,' he said.

I felt Dad jump.

'Ah, the little man.' He held out his hand. 'What have you drawn me — another monster?'

Jack shook his head. Dad took the picture, turned his head one way and then the other.

'What is it?'

'It's the tall building on the hill . . . where you work,' Jack said.

'We watched you,' I said, 'through my binoculars.'

His head twitched twice, then he blinked five times, slowly, like a pigeon. He'd spent all day in the building but still didn't seem to know what it was.

He mumbled something and I asked him what he'd said. He looked out the window, then towards the front door.

'It's a secret,' he said. 'They might be listening.' He put a finger in front of his lips.

Jack sat down beside me. Dad nodded at the picture.

'It's the cosmodrome . . .' he whispered. 'It's where I learn Russian . . . It's where I do my training.'

I told him we'd watched him from the hill and that we'd waited for him to come out. He pointed at one of the windows in Jack's picture and told us that was the room he'd been in, that whilst he was running on a machine he'd waved because he knew we were watching. I told him that we hadn't seen him and wondered if there was something wrong with my binoculars. He told me to go and get them.

I ran upstairs and found them in their case under my bed. As I went back down the stairs I looked through them the wrong way. The front door was so small I felt like a giant and when I got to the living room Jack looked like a dwarf waving at me on the settee. I laughed and waved back, then scanned along past two orange cushions and found Dad with his eyes closed. I had so many questions to ask him about the cosmodrome, what he did there, who else worked there with him, but I couldn't ask him now because as I looked through my binoculars it was like he was asleep at the end of a long tunnel.

Dad had been asleep for ten minutes when Mum came in and said dinner was ready. He opened his eyes, said he wasn't hungry, that he'd eaten lots of energy food and pills. Mum turned the TV down, went back out into the kitchen and brought our dinner in on trays. Me and Jack started eating, Dad picked up his fork and tapped it on his knee. And when Mum went back out to get the salt he mashed his potatoes and hid the liver underneath.

'Sporry wurry sputnik,' he whispered.

I didn't understand. I pushed my head closer to his and he put his hand on my shoulder.

'Sporry wurry sputnik . . . I learnt it today.'

'What does it mean?' I asked.

'I don't know,' he said. 'I just learnt how to say it, they tell me what it means next week.'

'Who?'

He looked out the window, then back at the sitting-room door.

'The Russians,' he said.

'The Russians?'

'Shush.' He put his finger up to his lips. 'Top-secret.'

I shuffled closer to him until my head bumped against his shoulder.

'Dad, why's it top-secret?'

He looked out the window and at the door again, then pulled me and Jack close to him. His eyes were open wide, his pupils were small and the whites were red at the edges.

'I'm going to the moon,' he whispered.

I heard a ringing noise like someone had knocked me on the head. I looked at Jack; his jaw was hanging and his eyes were as wide as Dad's. Dad pulled us closer. I felt the warmth of his breath on my face.

'Tell no one,' he said. 'Top-secret.'

I felt my heart beat faster. I had hundreds of questions before and I had even more now, but they all wanted to come out at the same time.

Jack closed his mouth then opened it again.

'Can we go too?'

Dad looked straight ahead.

Jack tapped him on the shoulder.

'Dad, can we go too?'

But Dad didn't seem to be listening, he just looked between us into space and started blinking so many times that I lost count. It was like all the new information the Russians were giving him was battling to get into his brain and then having a fight inside. I put my hand on his.

'Dad?'

He leant forward. Me and Jack looked at each other then moved out of the way. Dad stared straight ahead at the TV screen.

There were soldiers standing by a shop on a corner, they swivelled their guns and aimed them right at us. Green army trucks passed by, people were running around wearing black uniforms and balaclavas. Four helicopters hovered in the sky. We watched as the Union Jack burnt and green flags fluttered. Jack nudged me, asked me if it was a war and which ones were the Germans. I didn't answer. I only knew the Union Jack was us, I didn't know about the green flag.

A man dressed in black stood on a pavement with a bottle in his hand. Behind him IRISH REPUBLICAN ARMY SAYS BRITISH TROOPS GO HOME was painted in big letters on a wall. The man stuffed a rag in the bottle and lit the top. I looked at Dad.

'Is that where you were fighting?' I asked.

Dad didn't answer, he just stared at the man running with the bottle. A flame was burning on the top. The man threw it. It flew through the air, smashed against a truck and the truck caught fire. I heard the bang of a bomb and the rattle of bullets. Dad jumped beside me, he clenched his fork and blinked like the bombs were going off inside his head. He started to shake.

'Dad, what's wrong?'

His eyes opened wide, his fork dropped onto his plate and his plate fell onto the floor. I stood up and ran towards the door. I shouted for Mum. I heard the cutlery crash in the kitchen and she ran in with soapy water dripping from her fingers. She looked at me. I looked at Dad. He was still staring at the TV.

'Steve,' she said. She stood between Dad and the TV. 'Steve!'

Dad shook his head like he'd just woken up.

'What?'

Mum turned the TV off then knelt down in front of him. Me and Jack stood side by side. We didn't know what we should do as they stared at each other without talking. Dad started to shiver.

'It's OK,' Mum said. 'Everything is OK.' She put her arm around him and helped him stand up. They walked across the room and went out into the hall. I could hear Dad talking as they went up the stairs.

'Sporry,' he said. 'Sporry wurry sputnik.'

Me and Jack looked at each other as the floorboards creaked above us. I switched the TV back on, turned the sound down. People were marching down the street, some carried green flags, some carried orange. They marched past the smouldering truck and the writing on the wall. A Union Jack was burning, all the soldiers had gone, and where a building once stood there was a pile of smoking rubble.

Me and Jack looked at each other. Our house was dark and quiet. Neither of us had ever been the last one up before. I looked at the table, at the dirty plates, at Dad's knife and fork stuck in the mound of mash potato. Jack got up from the floor and sat down next to me. We listened for more creaks in the ceiling but all we heard was the tick of the clock on the mantelpiece and the sound of a car engine humming up the hill. I reached under the settee and pulled out the book that Mum had given me. Jack sat close to me in the silence and I wondered if he was thinking the same as me. Our dad was going to the moon and we couldn't tell anyone about it, but at least we had a book where we could write it down.

The next morning me and Jack were playing football in the hall while Mum and Dad were talking in the kitchen. I went in goal and tried to listen as Jack took the penalties, but it was hard to hear their whispers above the noise of the dishes and our ball banging against the door. I could just make out Dad's words, I couldn't hear Mum's replies.

'I'll be leaving soon.'

Bang!

'A month.'

Bang!

'That's lunar, not calendar.'

Bang!

'Lunar, not calendar.'

Bang!

'It's T minus—'

Bang!

'Let me tell the boys.'

Bang!

'But—'

'I said, no.' Mum sounded like she was mad. 'I'll tell them. You just need to concentrate on yourself.'

I pressed my ear closer to the door. Jack stood next to me and did the same.

'I can't hear anything,' he said.

I listened harder but all I could hear was the sound of a tap dripping, Mum and Dad mumbling and Jack's breath wheezing in my ear.

'I think they're doing sex,' he said.

'In the kitchen?'

He started to giggle. He put his hand over his mouth and his eyes started to water. The giggles got louder, rapid bursts, like a machine gun with a muffler.

Ddddddddddddaaaaaaaaaaa! Ddddddddddddddaaaaaaaa!
Yes, it was just like that.

The door opened and we fell forward and landed on the kitchen floor.

Jack was still giggling. I was laughing. But when I looked up at Mum and Dad the silence stopped me. Dad was standing staring at the fridge, moving his finger along the calendar like he was counting the days left in June. Mum was staring out the window, nodding her head like she was counting the flowers in the garden.

The tap dripped.

Me and Jack got up. He stood by the sink next to Mum. I stood by the fridge next to Dad. We hadn't heard an argument but it was like we were choosing our sides just in case.

Dad was still looking at the calendar. I asked him what he was doing. He turned around and looked at me. His eyes were black like he had been punched in them twice.

'Counting the days,' he said.

'Until you leave?'

Dad looked at Mum. She picked a piece of potato peel up off the floor and put it in the sink.

'So when do you go?' I asked.

He twitched his head like a fly was buzzing in his ear. 'In T minus twenty-eight days, and . . .' he looked at his watch, 'T minus twenty-eight days, six hours, twenty-three minutes, twelve seconds and counting.'

'What does "T minus" mean?' Jack asked.

Dad stared at the floor like the answer was written on the tiles.

'It's complicated,' he said. 'I need to go to work. Tom will tell you.' He walked past Mum, sat on the back step and put his trainers on.

'But I don't know either,' I said.

Dad looked up at me. 'Why not look it up in your encyclopaedia?'

I ran upstairs and found it on my shelf next to my bed and then ran back to the kitchen. I flicked through the pages, past Oceans, past Volcanoes and stopped on Space . . . The Universe . . . Planet Constellations . . . I held my finger against Space Travel.

'What section will it be under?' I asked.

The wind blew through the door and turned the page.

I looked up for Dad to give me the answer but he had already gone.

Chapter Seven

The sun is so high in the sky that we don't follow it or leave it behind. We keep walking but with every stride it feels like our legs are melting into the ground. We kick stones along the road.

We pull branches from trees.

We get fat pieces of grass and blow them between our thumbs.

We pick blackberries from a bush.

I don't like—

We eat twenty and move on.

—

—

The grand old Duke of York. He had—

Do we have to sing that again?

It makes the time go quicker.

It doesn't.

We're hungry and we're thirsty. Our last meal was a piece of chewing gum, our last drink came from the trough. We're going our fastest but still moving too slowly and the roads twist and turn and never end, and—

The grand old Duke of York.

!

. . . He had 10,000 men.

And we have sung this song so many times that when we get to the top of this hill there will be a million soldiers waiting for us.

A road sign wriggles in the heat haze. We try to read it but the sun is too bright and sweat stings our eyes. We get closer – two arrows point in opposite directions:

← Pentyre 23
Sefton 25 →

We scratch our head. If we were birds we could look down and see the road that took the easiest route, the road that would scoot us around the hills instead of making us crawl over.

But we're not birds.

No.

So we have to walk?

Yes.

All the way?

——

And we can't turn back?

Never.

Because we killed the chicken?

!

We take our book out of our bag and try to find one of Dad's maps.

Found one!

That was quick.

I know. This is one of Dad's maps.

Sorry . . . not that one. Ha!

!

We open another piece of paper.

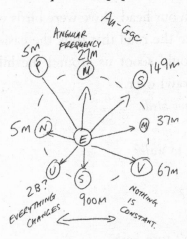

This is the first map Dad sent us. We used it the first time we tried to escape but all it did was send us in circles. He must have sent it for a reason but we don't know why because a map of the universe isn't much use when we're stuck on Earth. There are many things

Dad told us that we still can't work out. We thought it was because they were secrets, that maybe it was some kind of code that he sneaked in when he told us stories at night.

Stories about genies.

Secrets about Stalin.

Stories about elves.

Secrets about the atomic bomb.

Stories about Father Christmas.

Secrets about Hitler.

He told all these things at the same time. We didn't know what was made up or what was the truth.

I did.

You didn't.

I did.

Jack, just for once can you let me think on my own?

Sorry . . . It's not my fault.

I know.

We fold the map and put it back in our book and put our book in our bag.

———

———

. . . But Hitler was true.

. . . Yes, Hitler was true.

And Stalin.

Yes.

And Father Christmas.

And Father Christmas.

Ummm . . . no.

No? But I thought—

Didn't you notice that Father Christmas stopped
coming after Dad went to the moon?

—

—

We stand in front of the sign. We have been here ten
minutes and we still don't know which way to go.

That way.

That way.

We open our arms.

One . . . two . . . three.

What are you doing?

We lift up our hands.

One . . . two . . . three. Scissors.

Scissors.

Again.

I'm not playing.

I can cut you.

. . . I can cut you.

One . . . two . . . three.

Paper.

Paper.

You're copying me . . . Let me count this time.

Will it make a difference?

No, it's just my turn.

!

One . . . two . . . three!

Stone.

Stone.

One . . . two . . . thr— Police!

Police!

The sound of a siren pierces through the hills. We pick up our bag, run across the road and push our way into a hedge. The thorns scratch our arms and our back.

Ouch!

Shush!

The siren gets louder. Sweat runs down the side of our face as the noise runs around inside our head. An engine revs and a whoosh of air takes our breath. We peer out of the hedge as an ambulance flashes by.

—

—

That'll be for Frost.

What?

The ambulance.

Why?

—

Why, Jack?

It — it was an accident.

What have we done? All you had to do was tie him up while I jammed the window.

. . . But he woke up.

How?

141

When you smashed the glass. He started shouting . . . Then he started to wriggle.

So?

So I pulled the sheet tighter.

So he couldn't move?

Sort of . . .

Sort of?

He said he couldn't breathe.

What?

He said he couldn't breathe.

I said tie his feet, not his neck.

It wasn't my fault he was sleeping upside down.

Oh shit!

You shouldn't say—

Oh fuck!

Or that—

We put our hands on our head, turn round in circles. Our world goes dizzy, turns black at the edges.

Oh, Jack, what have we done? What have we done?

—

Oh shit. Oh shit!

But — it was you who killed the chicken.

We stop spinning, look at the sign. Whichever way we go, we have to go quickly.

We pick up our bag and walk in silence, with just the sound of our feet scuffing and our blood bumping in our head, trying to think, trying to think what we should do next.

We jump over a gate when we hear a car. We think of running when we hear a bus and when the ambulance flashes by with just its lights flashing we wonder if Frost is dead or alive.

. . . *I'm sorry.*

We're thinking.

It was an accident.

That's what we'll tell them if they catch us.

But they won't catch us.

—

Will they?

No . . . but we have to have a story. We'll tell them you didn't mean to do it.

Me! I thought we did everything together?

Not this.

?

We'll tell them it was an accident, that it can't be undone. We can't go back over the wall and untie all the knots . . . The knots!

?

You can't tie knots. You can't tie our shoelaces.

So?

You didn't do it. You couldn't have killed Frost.

But—

But what?

You taught me.

Shit!

143

—

That makes me an accomplice.

What does that mean?

It means we have to keep going.

Because we don't want to go to Houndsgate?

Because we don't want to go to prison.

!

!

We sling our bag over our shoulder and run along the road to Pentyre.

Chapter Eight

Is it much farther?

———

Is it much farther?
Further.
Is it much further?
I don't know.
Aaarh!
Ha!
!

We reach the crest of a hill. A house seems to grow out of the ground. A sign hangs from a pole:

THE BLACK SWAN PUBLIC HOUSE

We scuff our trainers through the dust and stones in the car park and look in through a window. Four men sit on stools in front of a bar, drinking pints and eating sandwiches. Our mouth starts to water. We lean closer until our nose hits the glass. One of the men turns round.

We duck down below the ledge.

Did he see us?

I don't think so.

We creep around the side of the pub. The door opens, the thud of music and the cackle of people laughing rush out. We crouch down behind a car and peer through the windows. A man in a suit comes out and walks towards us. We scurry across the shadow of the building and hide behind a stack of crates and boxes leant against a wall. A car door opens and closes, an engine starts and the car drives off.

We turn around and see the crates piled as high as we are tall, with wasps buzzing around bottle tops. We pick up a bottle, hold it up to the sun. Dregs swill in the bottom.

We can't—

We have to.

We tip our head back and drink. The cider is warm and tastes like water. We drink another, and another, until our thirst has gone and we remember our hunger. We open the boxes and search like tramps through bins but all we find are bottle tops and split packets of crisps.

They're soft.

They're cheese-and-onion.

They make me feel sick.

We stuff the crisps in our mouth and munch them up until our belly swells.

Our feet start to throb. We look around for

somewhere to sit but the ground is littered with shards of glass that glitter in the sun. We creep out and walk across the car park. At the end is a garden full of dandelions with a wheelbarrow in the middle and a rope swing that hangs from a tree.

Can we go on it?

No.

We walk through a gate and lie back in the long grass. When we close our eyes the world turns orange. The sun beats down on our body and warms us like we are lizards.

Everything is quiet.

Except for the puff of our breath.

And the thud of our heart.

And a fly buzzing in our ear.

We flick it away, put our hands behind our head and think about all the places we have been and all the places we want to go.

The beach.

The park.

Our hill. We remember sitting on top.

We remember playing our favourite game.

Oh no!

Can we play it now?

We can't.

Why not?

We've been drinking.

Can we try?

We pick up our book.

Oh good. You can drive.

Thanks.

We imagine we are on our hill. We imagine we are driving the bus to town. Our book is our steering wheel. Our pen is our indicator. We put our foot on the accelerator and pull away.

Wait!

What?

I've not got on yet.

!

—

Go on then.

There's a queue.

I've had enough.

It's OK, it's just a man with a hearing aid.

—

. . . And a lady with a baby.

—

. . . And a pushchair.

—

—

Are they on yet?

Yes.

We check our mirrors and drive through the park, under the trees, past the swings and along by the river.

I feel sick.

Because I'm driving too fast?

Because of the cider.

We put our book back on the ground and our pen in our bag. The drone of an aeroplane sounds overhead.

A DC-10?

A DC-10 McDougal Douglas.

McDonnell!

Is it?

I don't . . . I don't know.

The plane flies in a circle, gets quicker and quicker, until it turns over and over like a silver leaf tumbling from the sun.

Our mouth is dry, our head is dizzy and a cold sweat starts to trickle down our neck. We shake our head and hope the feeling will go away.

Why do you do that?

Because sometimes it works.

But I might fall out.

You'll never fall out.

Because the holes are too small?

Because I won't let you.

But they might take me.

They won't.

But they might.

I said they won't.

But—

I think you should stop worrying.

I wish we hadn't eaten the crisps.

I wish we hadn't drunk the cider.

We take deep breaths. In one second all our worries go away but in the next they come rushing back again:

Dad.

Mum.

Frost.

The chicken.

!

They run through our head and chase each other inside. Our stomach cramps, we clutch our hands against it. We kneel up. Our head starts to thud. Our throat starts to burn. We wrap our arms around our stomach and retch.

It tastes horrible.

I know.

We wipe cider and crisps from our mouth and lie back down. The world starts to spin.

You should go to sleep.

I'll try.

—

—

—

Our eyes flicker and grow heavy. The sound of a bird singing grows loud and disappears.

We yawn.

—

Jack?

—

Jack?

—

We look at the sky; the noise of the engine has disappeared and now the plane is just a little speck against the sun. Our head starts to ache. We screw up our eyes tight, try to make it go away. We want to go to sleep, but one of has to keep guard. The noise gets louder, we see flashing colours, red, green and purple, they spin around and turn into pictures of people that we want to forget. People in white coats. Dr Greenaway and Dr Anderson. They walk around and click their pens in a room with white walls and no windows.

—

Jack!

—

Jack, wake up.

—

There's a big grey machine beside us with dials on the front and wires trailing out. We look for a way out—

White wall. White wall. No windows. One door. Two doctors, three nurses, one porter and two security guards.

Jack, wake up!

—

I look at the ceiling, see slits of white light and shadows leaning over us.

Hands press on our head.

Fingers crawl over our skull.

I try to shout. We try to scream.

The fingers creep down to our jaw. We close our mouth. They prise it open and force a piece of rubber inside.

The rubber squeaks on our teeth and jams on our tongue. I spit it out, they put it back in. We shake our head from side to side.

'Hold still. Hold him still.'

Hands on my body, hands on our arms. They put a metal cage—

No—

They put a metal cage around our head that burns us hot and cold.

Dr Anderson leans over us and blocks out the light. He wears rubber gloves and has two wires in his hands.

'Steady. Steady.'

The wires come towards us.

We shake our head. We wriggle like worms.

Blue sparks flash—

We try to scream—

'It's for your own good. We're trying to make you better.'

We try to shout but our voice is smothered like we are trapped under a pillow.

A pair of scissors. A roll of tape. They cut two pieces and stick them down over our eyes.

'Stand clear.'

All the hands let go and we are left all alone.

—

A click.

A tickle.

An ant on the side of our head running in circles.

Jack, wake up now. Jack, wake up!

Our jaw clamps tight, our teeth sink into the rubber.

We hear a hum.

It gets louder and louder.

The tickle turns to an itch and then a buzz.

Buzz buzz. Buzz buzz.

We close our eyes and smell the electricity burn.

—

—

Tom?

—

Tom?

—

We open our eyes. Our body is shaking, our skin is wet with sweat and our temples are burning like the electricity is running through them now.

We sit up and take deep breaths.

Jack?

—

Jack?

—

We are glad only one of us remembers what happened, we are glad one of us is still sleeping.

We wish we could both sleep because our feet are aching like we have been walking barefoot all summer.

—

But we have to take it in turns, like . . .

Like we are soldiers.

Summer 1971

I didn't see Dad very much during the next week. Since he'd said he was going to the moon he seemed to be getting up earlier and earlier and coming home later and later, and as every day went past the summer seemed to be getting hotter and hotter. I had lots of questions to ask him – why was he training with the Russians? Why was he going to the moon? And what did T minus mean? But every night he came home wet with sweat and said he was tired. He'd only sit on the settee for five minutes before he went upstairs to bed.

I thought about it while I was at school every day. I thought about asking the teachers, but I wasn't sure I should say anything because Dad had said it was a secret.

On the last day of the week I couldn't wait any longer. I went to my first lesson. Mr Thomas wrote the date on the board and drew a Viking underneath. He told us to copy it, but no matter how long I stared or how many times I blinked, the only thing I could see were numbers ticking away in my head.

T minus twenty-eight days, six hours, twenty-three minutes, twelve seconds . . . and counting.

I put my hand up in the air.

'Mr Thomas,' I said. 'What does "T minus" mean?'

He narrowed his brow, looked at me, at the chalk in his hand and then at the Viking.

'This is Art, Tom,' he said. 'Not Maths, not Physics.'

I put my hand down, looked out the window. The first years were playing touch rugby in the playground. I wanted to run outside and join them, score a try and keep running out of the gate and all the way home.

I went to Geography. I went to History. I heard Mr Simms talking about riverbeds and valleys, abrasion and erosion. I heard Miss Bright talk about Hitler, how he built an army and invaded Poland. I heard all those things, but nothing went inside my head. When your dad says he's going to the moon you can't think of anything else. I just sat there staring at the clock, watching the minute hand jump, watching the hour hand crawl, thinking about getting back to Dad before the hours ran out at the end of another day.

There was a blue car parked outside our house when me and Jack got home. Two men in army uniform were standing on the front grass talking to Mum. Jack thought one of them was Dad. I told him that neither of them were, just that all soldiers looked the same when you saw them from a distance. Mum waved. The soldiers took off their hats. One had grey hair, the other had black. It was Tony and Geoff. They smiled as me and Jack got closer.

'Is this Jack?' said Geoff.

'It can't be,' said Tony.

'He's catching you up, Tom.'

Jack smiled, went on tiptoe, tried to make himself taller.

'He'll be able to beat you up soon.'

I felt myself go red.

Tony jabbed me in the ribs.

'Just kidding,' he said.

Me and Jack stood between them and they looked at Mum. Mum looked at me. We stood in silence. It was like I had done something wrong. I waited for Mum to say something to get me out of trouble, like she used to when Dad told me off for wearing his boots and getting them muddy in the middle of winter. She used to tell him I was only playing, that I'd help her clean the mud off, and we'd sit together on the back step to polish them back to new. This time Mum didn't say anything, she just smiled. But it wasn't her usual smile, it was a smile into space, like I wasn't even there.

I felt a tap on my shoulder.

'Here.' Tony gave me his hat and Geoff gave his to Jack. We put them on and ran off across the grass, grenades in our hands, bayonets and rifles strapped to our backs. We ran between parked cars, searched for camouflage cover, but I couldn't find anything black to match my school uniform. A man on a bike came along the road. I set up my sights on a wall. We waited for the man to get closer. Jack threw a grenade. I let fire with the bullets. The man wobbled on his bike.

'Got me,' he said.

Me and Jack laughed and waited for another enemy to come.

I looked back through my sights towards our house, tried to trace Tony, Geoff and Mum, but they had gone.

Me and Jack ran across the road, crept down our path, crouched as we went around the side of our house. Tony and Geoff were standing by the coal-shed door. We crept closer, slid our backs along the wall. Tony made a gun with his fingers.

'Too noisy,' he said. 'But give me my hat back and I'll let you surrender.'

Geoff shouted into the shed.

'We're off now, Steve.'

Dad didn't reply.

Tony took my hat, tapped me and Jack on the head.

'Be good soldiers,' he said.

I watched them walk around the corner. Jack tugged my arm.

'What's that noise?' he asked.

The noise stopped, then started again. Dad was sawing in the shed. We put our backs against the wall and crept to the shed door. Dad was in a dark corner with his head bent over. All I could see were his back and his shoulders, and his arm jabbing up and down as he cut the edges off a piece of wood. I put my bag outside and walked in. It was cool and dark inside. My foot kicked a piece of coal; it rolled across the floor towards him. He stopped, held up his arm and wiped sweat off his forehead.

'Dad,' I said. 'What are you doing?'

He jumped.

'Tom,' he said. 'I didn't hear you come in.' His face was red and sweaty. The saw was shaking in his hand.

Jack stepped out behind me.

'Ha! I didn't see you either.' Dad smiled and laid the saw on the ground.

'What are you doing?' I asked again.

He picked up two circles of wood the size of dustbin lids. 'Making clocks,' he said.

I looked at the circles. They had strange letters around the edges and the word 'Mockba' was written in the middle.

Dad laughed. 'It'll help you keep time,' he said. He took two batteries from his pocket, put them in a little box that he'd screwed to the backs of the clocks. I looked at Jack and smiled. All our friends had watchesbut none of them had their own clocks. Dad reached over to the bench.

'Carry these up to your bedroom,' he said.

He handed me a hammer and threw Jack a bag of nails. We ran out of the shed into the light. The air was hot and it was hard to breathe. It was getting hotter every day, like we were all locked in an oven. I felt one of the clocks nudge me in the back.

'Go on,' said Dad. 'I'll follow behind.'

Me and Jack walked along the path at the back of house and went inside.

Mum was washing up in the kitchen. She asked us where we were going.

'Dad's made us clocks,' I said.

'This big.' Jack held his hands out wide.

Mum smiled, but I don't think she believed us. I turned to run away. She wiped a plate, put it in the rack and then followed us upstairs.

I sat down next to Jack on his bed. Mum came in and sat in the middle between us. She put her arms around our shoulders and smiled. I thought that she looked as excited as us. We listened to Dad's footsteps on the stairs, then a thump, then a knock. Mum squeezed me tight as his shadow crept along the landing, the circles of the clocks in the middle of his body. Jack bounced up and down on the bed. Dad stood in the doorway and took a step towards us. The clocks knocked against the frame of the door.

'Sporry,' he said. 'I think I've made them too big.'

Jack laughed. Dad tried again, but he couldn't get in, he was like a cartoon cat trying to chase a mouse through a hole. Mum got up and walked towards him. He turned the clocks and came through the door sideways. His head bashed against our planes that hung by fishing wire from the ceiling. Dad grinned and I think he winked, but he'd started to blink so much that I couldn't be sure. Mum held the clocks while he climbed onto Jack's bed. I gave him the hammer, Jack gave him a nail. He banged it into the wall next to Jack's Chelsea poster and hung the clock on top. Then I pulled down my Arsenal poster and he hung the other clock on mine.

I sat on my bed and watched my clock, but something was wrong – the second hand was going backwards. I looked at Jack's – his was going backwards as well. I thought about telling Dad, but it had taken him all afternoon to make them, I didn't want him to know they were broken. He walked over to the window, looked up at the sky and then at his wrist.

'We're synchronised,' he said.

'What does that mean?' asked Jack.

Dad looked at me like he was expecting me to say something,

but since the clocks were going backwards I wasn't sure of the answer. He held out his arm. Me and Jack got off our beds and stood beside him. I pulled his arm towards me. His watch hung loose on his wrist, the gold strap had scratches that glistened in the sun and there was a crack across the glass that joined the number 2 to the number 9. Dad pointed his finger at the second hand as it swept over the number 6 towards the 5.

'But Dad,' I said, 'it's going backwards. And our clocks are going backwards.'

He looked at our clocks, then back at his watch.

'I know . . . I know.' He scratched his head. 'That's what T minus . . . That's what T minus . . .' He repeated it again but still didn't answer. He was like one of my robots when it had run out of battery. Mum took him by the arm. He smiled and they walked towards the door. Me and Jack looked at each other, then back at him.

'But Dad,' I said, 'I still don't know what T minus—'

Dad's head was pointed towards the ground. Mum stopped and looked over her shoulder.

'Later, Tom,' she whispered. 'Dad will tell you later.'

I listened to the creaks on the floorboards as they went along the landing and then down the stairs. I looked at Jack; he was staring at my wall, swinging his feet over the side of his bed. There was no echo of the radio in the kitchen, there was no rumble of the TV through the floor, there was just the occasional whisper of Mum's voice, the rumble of Dad's, and the tick-tick-tick as the hands of our clocks crawled like insects up the wall.

* * *

In the evening, after we'd eaten, Dad took us outside. We followed him past the shed around the side of the house and out onto the front path. The air was warm and insects were buzzing over the sound of our footsteps and the distant boom of Mr Green's TV.

Dad sat down on the ground and tapped the grass with his hand. Me and Jack lay down beside him and used his chest as a pillow. My head went up and down when he breathed and when he spoke his words rumbled through his body.

'Look at the sky,' he said.

I looked up and watched the sky turn orange as the sun went down behind the hill and the moon came over the top of our house. It was bigger and brighter than I'd ever seen it before. I wanted to ask Dad why but every time I went to open my mouth I felt a sigh build in his chest.

I heard a police siren in the distance.

Streets of San Francisco?
No.
Kojak?
—

It faded away when Mr Green closed his window.

We lay on the grass in silence. I looked across at Jack, his eyes were closed. A line of dribble trailed from his mouth, down his cheek and made a dark patch on Dad's shirt.

I heard footsteps. Dad pulled me tighter to him as Mum walked along the path and stood in front of the moon. I couldn't see her face but I could hear her voice. It was really quiet, like she was in church. She bent down towards Jack.

'Do you want me to take him?'

Dad shook his head, and his head shook his body, and I felt a single word rumble through his chest.

'No.'

Mum took off her cardigan and wrapped it around Jack, then kissed him, then me, then Dad.

She walked away down the steps.

I looked back up at the sky. The moon was nearly white with just a little dark patch of yellow on one side and a smaller patch at the bottom. I wondered why it was so big, why it was so white and why the stars seemed to hang from strings just like our planes from our bedroom ceiling. Jack made a groaning noise and rolled over.

'It's an elliptical orbit,' Dad whispered, so close that his breath seemed to burn my ear. He leant closer. 'That's why the moon seems bigger.'

A shiver grew inside me, made chicken bumps on my arms. I turned my head, felt him smile in the dark, and I wondered how he could watch the sky and read my mind at the same time. I kept staring at the sky, at the brightness of the stars, at the darkness in between, and I wondered how fast his rocket would go, whether I would be able to see him, what it would be like to float, and how long he would be gone for.

'Seventeen thousand five hundred miles per hour,' he whispered.'. . . In the mornings on TV, in the sky at night. Don't know . . . Oh, and I'll be gone for twenty-eight days.'

I asked him how he would breathe, how he would sleep and where he would pee.

'Oxygen tanks. Strapped down. In my spacesuit.'

I laughed. His body shook and made me laugh longer and when I stopped everything seemed quieter than it had been before. I rolled over, put my chin on his chest and asked him the question that had been bothering me the most, the question that had been in my head all week.

'Dad,' I said, 'what does T minus mean?'

'It's easy,' he said. 'I'll show you.'

He lifted up his hand and I followed his finger as he drew a big circle around the moon.

'Imagine the moon is a clock,' he said. 'Imagine it's a clock, an alarm clock inside your head.'

'But the bell will never go off,' I said.

He laughed. 'No,' he said. 'But my rocket will.'

He put his hand under his elbow, pivoted his arm into the sky and told me it was the clock's second hand moving backwards. He said every second it moved backwards was a second closer to lift-off, and when it reached sixty, the minute hand would tick back and it would start all over again. I told him I understood but that we shouldn't tell Jack because he hadn't learnt to tell the time forwards yet. Dad laughed and we put our heads back on the grass and looked up at the sky.

Then he told me about the satellites.

He told me about Echo, how it sends radio signals back from space. He told me about Tiros, that it takes pictures of all of the oceans and the wind patterns and then sends them back to Earth so we can predict the weather. And he told me about the militaries in America and Russia, how they tell everyone they are looking for new planets but really they are watching each other.

'Like spies?' I asked.

'Yes,' he said.

'Are you going to be a spy?'

'No,' he said. 'I can't keep a secret.'

I laughed. Dad sighed and everything went quiet again.

My legs started to twitch, my back began to ache. I rolled over on my side and he hugged me so tight I couldn't move. He told me that while he was gone the days would get hotter and longer and that he would spend them thinking about me and Jack. I told him twenty-eight days was a long time, maybe I could call him.

'No,' he said. 'There aren't any telephone boxes in space.'

'Walkie-talkies then?'

He smiled. 'No, they'll be out of range . . . But I'll have a radio.'

'Great,' I said.

He screwed up his face and rapped his knuckles on his head. 'Bugger it! Oops! Sporry . . . but I forgot, we'll lose the signal when I go around the dark side of the moon.'

He started to mumble. I couldn't tell if I was meant to hear or if he was talking to himself. I felt him shake. I sat up and looked at him. His mouth moved but no words came out and I wondered how I would be able to communicate with him when he was 238,857 miles away, if I couldn't understand him when he was by my side.

An idea came into my head in the dark. I tapped my hand on his chest. 'I've got it,' I said.

He jumped.

'What?'

'How we can communicate when you're in space.'

He sat up, looked up and down the road, then back at our house.

'Whisper it,' he said. 'We don't want the spies to hear.'

'Letters,' I whispered. 'We could send letters.'

He bit his lip like he wasn't sure.

'I could send you one. You could send me one back. All we have to do is decide who writes first.'

'You'll be too busy writing your book to write to me.'

I told him I wouldn't, that if the days were going to get longer like he said, I would have time to write both. I laughed because he laughed.

He lifted his hand and rubbed my head and I watched a million stars reflect in his eyes.

'OK,' he said. 'I'll write first. I'll send you a letter from the moon.'

Chapter Nine

We hear the sound of tyres on gravel. The sun burns into our eyes and makes us blind. We smell petrol fumes, they burn up our nostrils into our head. Our stomach cramps but we have been sick so many times that there is nothing left inside.

An engine revs as a lorry reverses against the wall where we ate and drank. We slide back down into the long grass as the driver kills the engine and climbs down from the cab.

He's wearing a balaclava.

He's got a beard that joins up with his hat.

The driver walks to the side of the lorry, pulls back the blue canopy and ties it against the metal frame. A man in a checked shirt comes out of the pub. He shakes hands with the lorry driver, they walk across the yard and start to roll a barrel. They say something about it being hot, something about cricket and the driver says he's glad this is his last call of the afternoon. Together they lift the last barrel up onto the lorry and then they disappear into the Black Swan.

We stand up. Our head spins. We drop down to our knees and crawl through the grass.

Like Marines.

Like snakes.

What are we doing?

Hitching a ride.

Shouldn't we ask?

Dressed like this?

We look down at our clothes. Our shoes are dusty, our trousers are covered in sick and our T-shirt is splattered in blackberry stains and dirt.

We run through the dust and climb into the lorry. It's full of crates and barrels with ropes stretched across tying them together. We duck under and start to crawl, cold puddles of beer soak into our trousers and the further we go, the stronger it smells, the darker it gets. At the back of the truck we curl up on a bed of sacks and rags in the corner.

Like a cat.

Like a dog.

We stink.

I know.

And I'm scared.

It's OK.

We hear footsteps outside on the gravel. Everything around us shakes as the driver climbs in and starts the engine. The lorry lurches forward, a crate topples over, bottles fall out and smash on the floor beside us. We

squeeze ourself into the corner. The lorry stops. We
hear the door open and the driver say Fuck.

!

___

The truck rocks like a boat as he climbs up.

'Much damage?'

'Two crates.'

'Need a brush?'

'I've one in the back.'

We look around. The brush is beside us, jammed
between crates and barrels.

Shall we move?

He'll see us.

Footsteps thud through the floor towards us. We slide
the brush down onto the floor, pull a sack out from
underneath us and put it over our head. It makes our
head itch.

It stinks of petrol.

It smells of smoke.

!

We curl up in a ball and hope we don't catch fire.

The footsteps scuff closer.

Pray.

?

Pray.

Our Father . . .

In our head!

Oops!

Shall I put our hands together?

!

The footsteps grow louder. We screw up our eyes shut.

God, help me.

God, help him.

God, help us.

The shuffle of shoes stops by our side.

Oh no.

Oh fuck.

'Oh bollocks, I can't find the brush . . .'

—

—

'Use mine?'

Use his.

Use his.

'Nah! I'll do it back at the depot.'

The footsteps move away.

—

—

We pull the sack off our head and get our breath as the driver moves out of the darkness into the sun.

The truck moves across the gravel and bumps out onto the road. The barrels rock, the crates shake and every time they do, we know we are turning another corner, travelling along roads that take us further away from the place where we were trapped for so long.

We are tired.

We are happy.

Because we're going to the beach to find Dad.

Yes.

—

We just hope . . .

What?

We just hope we're going the right way.

Chapter Ten

Can we play We spy?

—

Can we?
Do we have to?
. . . We spy with our little eye something beginning with—
Hedge.
Yes. Your turn.

—

Your turn.
. . . We spy with our little eye, something—
House. My go.
!
We spy with our—
Field. We spy—
Horse.
I don't think this is working.
No.

Chapter Eleven

We have bumped over bridges. We have slid on the corners. The engine has stopped now and the driver has gone. We don't know how long we have been in here or how far we have travelled, only that the sun was shining when we left and now it is dark.

We slip our bag over our shoulder and crawl like rats under the ropes. The wind blows, sucks the canopy in and out. We hold our breath and wait for it to stop. A line of light shines in, stretches across the floor and cuts the trailer in half. We peer through the gap and see lorries parked bumper-to-bumper across a yard. A forklift truck with its orange light flashing raises its forks and rests them against two wooden gates.

To stop us getting out.

To stop thieves getting in.

But we're not thieves.

No.

A man climbs out, lights a cigarette, then disappears through a little door cut in the gate. A car door slams shut, an exhaust rumbles, then fades away. We feel our heart beat and the cold of the wind on our ears.

The light goes out and we are left alone with the moon.

We jump down and walk between the lorries. Some of them are attached to trailers, some of them stand on their own, all of them have fluorescent numbers that float in the dark.

Number twelve . . . number fifteen . . .

We haven't got time to count them.

We walk towards where the light came from and climb the metal stairs up the side of a building—

A bright light flashes. We put our hand over our eyes.

Halt!

Germans!

Who goes there?

We do.

Put your hands up.

No.

Surrender.

Run!

Ha!

?

We look up at the light. Night-bugs buzz as they fly around it, a little red sensor blinks by the side.

Sensors.

So it's not Germans?

No.

!

Ha!

We walk along the platform, stop by a window, take off our jumper and wrap it around our fist.

Ready?

I thought we weren't thieves.

We're not. We just want somewhere to sleep.

We punch the glass. The window rattles but we haven't even made a crack. We wrap our fist again and wonder why windows are so much easier to smash when we are trying to break out and not in.

Maybe it's because we don't hit them hard enough.

Maybe it's because we hit them harder when we are being chased.

We smack our fist again. The glass cracks loud like an iceberg. We lift the latch, climb through onto a table. Our hand knocks against a radio, our knee bangs against a typewriter.

It hurts.

Rub it.

I am . . . Oh, a typewriter!

I just said that.

Can we type our names?

No.

J . . . J . . . I can't find the J.

!

We drop our bag on the floor and stand in the middle of the room surrounded by darkness. We feel like we shouldn't be here, like we are in a church or a classroom after the bell has rung and everyone else has gone home.

There's a kettle, mugs and half a packet of biscuits on top of a fridge and a big map of Great Britain pinned to the wall. We walk towards it, knock our leg against a table, kick over a bin. We jump.

Sorry.

Sorry.

We stop and listen.

What is it?

Shush . . . It's OK.

The fridge switches on, rattles a spoon in a mug.

We walk on and stand in front of the map. Little pins are stuck in all the big cities and ports with dotted lines connecting them to the centre of the map.

Derby?

That's where we are, now all we have to do is find where we want to go.

We hold up our hand, put our finger on Derby and follow a line across England and into Wales—

Tom.

We're busy.

But—

Our finger stops on the pin stuck in the middle of Swansea with the number 9 written underneath.

?

It's the numbers on the lorries.

So people know where they're going?

Yes.

Like buses?

Yes.

Tom.

What is it?

Our hand's bleeding.

Shit!

We turn around and walk back to the window. Blood oozes from a cut, trickles across our knuckles, glistens under the spotlight. We search the room for something to wrap it in, but all we find is a rag that smells of coffee and lots of paper and files.

And three pencils.

—

And a stapler.

—

And a rubber . . . Can I keep—

No.

We sit on a table, wrap our hand in the sleeve of our jumper and squeeze it tight under our arm. It starts to throb. We rock backwards and forwards and try to make the pain go away. The wind blows through the window, blows the papers off the desk, rustles the map on the wall. The light goes out, all we can see are shapes and shadows. We shiver and try to hug ourself warm.

It's cold.

Like every room we've lived in for the last six years.

Except for the Harrisons'.

—

They had electric blankets.

The Harrisons were nice.

They were like all the others.

?

People we trusted who turned out to be traitors.

We lie back against the wall and think of all the other traitors we trusted. The Joneses—

The Harrisons.

We said them.

The lady at the bus stop?

—

. . . And the man at the clinic.

That was your fault, you shouldn't have kicked him.

He said he was getting a plaster, not sticking a needle up our bum.

—

We keep thinking, and the more we think, the more we realise that we can't trust anyone any more.

Except Dr Smith.

?

Do we think he's a traitor?

I don't know.

But he gave us a present.

—

Can we open it?

We pick up our bag and try to open it but it's hard to pop a popper when we can only use one hand. We

pull it open with our teeth and turn our bag upside
down. Our rockets and planes slide out onto the desk.
We pick up the little box that Dr Smith gave us.

Happy Birthday.

Happy Birthday.

*Happy birthday to us. Happy birthday to us. Happy
birthday dear—*

I think you can stop now.

Because we haven't got a cake.

——

Or candles.

Because you're giving us a headache.

Shall I put the light on?

No. It's too risky.

We wave our hand out the window.

I said—

The light comes back on.

!

——

We bite the tape with our teeth and rip away the
paper until all we are left with is a little white box.

What is it?

Don't know.

We lift the lid and look inside but all we see is pieces
of tissue paper.

It's a hamster!

——

They never let us have hamsters.

It's not a hamster.

We push the tissues away until we feel something hard and cold. We pick it up and hold it to the light. A tiny silver aeroplane shines between our fingers.

It's got a big nose.

It's Concorde.

We turn it in the air, bank left and right, climb and dive.

And fire the guns.

It hasn't got guns.

—

Just passengers.

Oh.

—

Is that all there was?

!

We look back in the box and find a piece of paper folded to the size of our nail. We open it up and read the tiny scrawly writing.

Dear Tom and Jack,
    Hope you like Concorde.
    Be safe, be careful, and stay out of the water.
    Dr Smith

We think of Dr Smith and wish we could have met him before in a different place, because he didn't just ask questions like all the others. He wasn't a traitor who couldn't be trusted. He listened to us, he told us to think, he told us to remember everything, every detail, that one day—

Everything will be quiet . . . and we can write the last chapter.

———

Can we write it now . . . on the typewriter?
No.

———

It's not quiet yet.
?

———

We yawn.
We're tired.
Are we?
Yes.

We rub our hands over our face. Our eyelids are so heavy that we cannot keep them up with our thumbs. We rest our head against the wall and put our feet up on the desk and look down at the shadows of the lorries parked side by side in the dark. Tomorrow we will be on number 9.

Tomorrow we're going to the beach.

Yes. Because it's where Dad used to take us, it's where he was happy. Sometimes people go back to the places that made them happy.

Like elephants?
?

Like elephants?

No.

But I thought . . .

No, they go back to places to die.

——

——

Our blood throbs in our hand. We are tired and cold.

But we're safe?

Yes.

And no one will come and take me?

No.

How do you know?

Because no one else could put up with your questions.

——

——

So we can read?

. . . We have to.

. . . *Can we read about the last time we went to the beach with Mum and Dad?*

OK.

And then I'll go to sleep.

And I'll keep guard.

Like a dog.

Like a wolf.

Hoooooooowlllllll!

Ha!

Ha!

We wrap ourself tight, let our head drop and rest on our shoulder. We breathe and go to sleep with one eye closed and the other watching the moon. It shines through the window, casts our shadow on the table, makes the shards of glass glisten, lights our fingerprints around the pane. We'll have to wipe them off in the morning, along with our blood. We don't want to leave a mess, we don't want to leave any traces of our DNA.

We look back up at the moon, see its oceans and craters, its eyes and its nose. We feel small and wonder why someone we want to see so much went so far away. Tomorrow we will be on the beach, one step further away from the house, one step closer to him. The wind blows across the glass, the red brake lights of a car wind through the hills. Our book falls down onto our lap.

We close our eye and hope that in the morning, when it opens, we will wake up with the sun.

Summer 1971

I was on the sand dune.

Mum was on the beach.

Jack was in the water.

Dad was in the rock pools with his space helmet on, stepping from one pool to another. Every once in a while he bent down, dipped his hand in the water and dropped something into a yellow plastic bag.

He stepped out from the shadow of the cliffs and turned towards me. The sun sparkled on his visor. I waved to him. He put his hand in the air and signalled for me to come over.

I slid down the dune, ran along the beach between the windbreaks and children building sandcastles.

He had moved on to another pool by the time I reached him.

'Dad,' I said, 'what are you doing?'

He didn't answer. He just turned and I saw myself reflected in his visor as he checked up at the cliff top, then back along the beach. Everything was quiet, like I was watching TV without sound.

'Nobody's watching, Dad,' I said. 'Nobody's listening.'

'There,' he said.

I followed the line of his finger as he pointed out to sea, beyond the wooden wave breaks, past a man rowing in a dinghy. I looked as far as I could see, to where there seemed to be a trail of black smoke behind the silhouette of a ship on the horizon. Dad tapped the side of his helmet.

'They might be watching,' he said. 'They might be spies.'

I stood watching the ship, wondering if there might be spies on board, but even if there were, I was sure they couldn't see us if I couldn't see them. I turned around to tell Dad, but he had moved on.

I climbed into the next pool where Dad was standing with one of his hands closed tight. He told me to hold the yellow bag. It rattled when I took it and was really heavy. Dad slowly unfurled his hand and, as I leant forward to get a better look, my head bumped against his helmet.

'Sporry,' he said.

I rubbed my head and watched as he brushed grains of sand off his palm with his finger until all that was left were three black dots in the middle.

'What are they?' I asked.

'Samples,' he whispered. 'Meteorite and moon dust, and there's more in there.'

I opened the bag wide and he dug his hand right to the bottom. 'There,' he said. 'Right there . . . anorthosite and breccias . . . and volcanic glass . . . !'

I looked closer but all I could see were shells, rocks, and a piece of seaweed wrapped around the tip of his finger.

'It's just beach things,' I said.

He nodded at the boat on the horizon.

'That's what they want you to believe,' he whispered, 'but that's not what the Russians have taught me.' He blinked and made a noise like a tape playing backwards. I bent down and scooped more sand from the water.

By the time we reached the ninth pool the bag was cutting into my fingers. Dad took it from me, tied the handles and then placed it on the sand. He said we could collect it later. The sun was burning my head, my skin was stiff with salt. I told him I was hot and thirsty. He nodded over my shoulder, said I needed to keep up because we were being followed. I looked back and saw a line of children; they were picking up things Dad had discarded and putting them in their buckets. I heard a girl say she was collecting meteorites. I heard a boy tell her she was collecting rubbish. I tried to keep up with Dad but the pools were getting rockier and deeper. I stopped for a rest. Someone tapped me on the shoulder. I turned around and saw a boy wearing a yellow T-shirt. He was taller than Jack but not as tall as me.

'Is your dad a scientist?' he asked.

'No,' I said.

I went to walk away. He tapped me on the shoulder again.

'What is he then?'

I looked at Dad, then back at the boy. 'He's a cosmonaut,' I whispered. 'He's going to the moon, but don't tell anyone else.'

The boy screwed his eyebrows together.

'What's a cosmonaut?'

I checked back at Dad; he was bent over with his hand deep in the water.

'They're the same as an astronaut except they come from Russia, not America.'

Dad stood up and took off his helmet. His hair was stuck down flat against the sides of his head and his face looked long and tired. He waded through the water towards me and the boy.

'Tom,' he said, 'I said not to tell anyone. They're out there listening.' His eyes seemed to pop out of his head as he pointed to the boat on the horizon.

I turned around to tell the boy but he was gone and the rock pool was empty. I looked up and saw the blur of his yellow T-shirt as he ran across the sand with all the girls trailing behind. I looked back at Dad.

'I'm sorry,' I said.

'What for?'

'Because I told them.'

He smiled.

'It's OK,' he said. 'It's OK.' He walked towards me and sat down on a rock.

I looked out at the water but I wasn't really looking at anything, I was just wishing I hadn't let out the secret, thinking that I should have kept my mouth shut. I felt an elbow in my ribs, looked up and saw Dad smiling with his helmet in his hands.

'Here,' he said. 'Try it on.' He held it over my head, pushed it down and clipped the strap under my chin. My head fell forward and the visor shut over my face. The sand turned orange, the sea turned black. I smelt sweat and leather. I tried to stand up but my head started to wobble. Dad started to laugh. I took a step, he held out his arms and stopped me falling over. He held me tight and the visor steamed up as my laughter echoed inside.

'My head's too big for my body,' I said.

'Or your body's too small for your head.' Dad smiled and helped me take the helmet off. I sat beside him. He laughed again, then went quiet as we watched Jack playing in the water as the sun moved across the sky.

I started to think of the clocks on the wall, ticking the time away at home. I thought how exciting it was that Dad was going to the moon, but the more I thought, the longer we sat together on the rock, the more I realised that I didn't want him to go.

His arm suddenly jumped on my shoulder. I looked up at him, his face twitched and a blue vein bulged in his neck. I asked him if he was OK. He said he felt a little dizzy, that maybe the sun was too hot or he hadn't drunk enough water. He bent over and held onto a rock. His skin pulled tight across his back and I counted the bumps where his ribs met his spine. I hadn't seen his ribs before. I hadn't noticed he was getting skinny. I also hadn't noticed the two red marks at the top of his neck.

He started to shiver. I asked him if he was cold. He shook his head.

'No,' he said. '. . . It's a trick the Russians taught me to lower my body temperature if I get too hot in space.' He blew out his cheeks. 'It's working,' he said. 'I feel cooler already.'

The vein on his neck started to disappear but the two marks were still there.

'Dad,' I asked, 'what are those marks?'

'What marks?'

'Those.' I pointed.

He jumped away from me and covered the marks with his hand.

'Oh, these? . . . They're from the electrodes . . . It's what they use to monitor my DOS.'

He looked along the beach, said Mum was waving for us to go and get some tea. I looked for Mum, but she wasn't waving, she was just sitting on a blanket on the sand. I looked back at Dad. I told him I could see two more marks on his chest.

He waved his hand like he was trying to brush off a wasp.

'Bloody electrodes,' he said. 'They get everywhere.'

I smiled but I didn't know why, maybe it was just because he did. He held out his hand and we walked down to the water to get Jack. On the way he told me how the Russians connected him up to a machine when he was running so they could see his heartbeat on a screen. I asked him what it looked like. He said it was like valleys and mountains; when his heart didn't beat he was at the bottom, when it did he was at the top, and the faster he ran, the bigger the mountains got until the valleys disappeared in between.

'So it's not a picture of your heart?' I asked.

He laughed. 'No, Tom,' he said. 'It's just a jagged line.' He rubbed my head and I felt like Jack must have done most of the time.

'Sporry wurry sputnik' he said.

'Sporry wurry sputnik,' I said back.

I laughed, but I still didn't know what it meant.

The water splashed against our legs as we walked out into

the sea and we reached Jack bobbing up and down between the waves. Dad put his helmet on his head and his hands down by his sides. I took one hand and Jack took the other. Dad started to walk parallel to the beach, dragged us faster and faster. I looked across at Jack, he was laughing and smiling. We kicked our legs out behind us and cut like sharks through the water.

When Dad got tired we turned towards the land and walked along the sand, past the lifeguard, until we stopped near the end where the yellow and red flags hung from poles. Dad put his hand on my shoulder and pointed at the sky.

'Tell me what you see,' he said.

I looked across at Jack. He shrugged. Dad pressed his hand down on my shoulder.

'Come on, Tom,' he said. 'I know you see it too.'

I told him I could see people standing on the cliff tops, that I could see seagulls swooping above them.

He shook his head like I was wrong.

'I don't know, Dad. I don't know what I'm supposed to see.'

He knelt down between me and Jack and held out his hand like it was a bird of prey hovering in the air.

'Imagine you're floating . . . across the sand, under the sun, over the dunes . . .'

'Like we're in a spaceship,' said Jack.

'Yes, Jack. Like we're in a spaceship.'

Jack smiled and looked at me. I wished I'd said that.

Dad pulled us closer to him. 'Imagine we have rockets,' he whispered. 'Imagine that we have rockets that are so powerful they can blast you off the Earth, but are as gentle as the breeze so you can land without a bump.'

I imagined myself hovering. I imagined the engines underneath. I looked across at Jack, he was hovering with me, with his eyes screwed up against the sun.

Dad pointed to the blue sky above the cliff top.

'Can you see the dust cloud?'

'Yes.'

'Yes.'

'Start the engine, Jack. Press the button.'

Dad flipped his visor down. I saw my reflection with Jack standing beside me; our bodies were small like babies, our heads were big like Martians.

Jack held up his finger and asked me which button.

'The middle one,' I said.

'This one?'

'Yes.'

The engines started and we rose into the sky. Jack held the wheel, Dad controlled the engines and I plotted our position out of the window. We travelled over the ridges and craters, the mounds and the hollows that were as wide as our sky and as deep as our oceans.

Jack turned left as Dad gave more boost to our engines. We flew over the Sea of Tranquillity, over catenae, dorsa, rimae and dustbowls and valleys that Dad didn't tell us the names of.

I felt water around my feet. Jack's arms started to shake. I waited for Dad to take over the controls and fly us home. But he was quiet, now he was just a passenger sitting in the seat behind us. He leant forward, put his head between ours and whispered so quietly it could have been the waves.

'I'll be going soon.'

I turned around and felt sad and excited at the same time. It was T minus one day, six hours and counting, but from the darkness I saw in his eyes it was like he hadn't just shown us the moon, he was already on it.

We looked up at the sky, at a flock of birds flying across the sea towards the red strips of cloud on the horizon. Dad mumbled, something about shepherds, something about mackerel. I told him I couldn't hear him. He mumbled again, and I caught the words 'tomorrow', 'wind speed' and 'nitrogen'.

I told him I didn't want him to go. Jack said he didn't want him to go, either. Dad's eyes went dark and sparkled. He told me to be good and to look after Jack. I told him I always was and I would. Then he went quiet. I felt water rushing around my feet. I tugged his arm.

'Dad,' I said, 'the tide's coming in.'

He didn't move, his helmet didn't move, it was like he had gone to sleep inside.

I looked at Jack, his face was white, his lips a thin line of blue.

The world went cold.

We stood together and shivered as we watched the sun go down in Dad's visor.

There were shadows outside my bedroom door when I woke up the next morning. I heard Dad cough, smelt smoke, soap and aftershave. When he bumped his head going down the stairs I heard Mum telling him to shush and not to wake the boys.

I knelt up in my bed and pulled back the curtain – everything looked cold and grey outside. Mum walked up the path carrying Dad's bag. Dad dragged his suitcase behind her. He was wearing a coat that I'd only seen in the winter. I reached behind me and wrapped myself warm in my blanket. Mum and Dad stopped under an orange street light at the end of the path.

A mattress spring pinged and made me jump. The curtain moved and I looked along the windowsill and saw Jack grinning at me from the other end.

'Is it Christmas?' he whispered.

'No.'

'But it feels like it?'

'Yes.'

My breath misted the window. I wiped it away. A car's head-lights lit up Mum and Dad as it turned into the road. A yellow taxi stopped beside them under the light. Dad picked up his suitcase, put it in the boot, put his helmet on and got inside. I watched the red lights shine bright as the taxi went to the top of the hill, turned around and came back down again. Mum waved, me and Jack waved too, but it was too dark to see if Dad was waving back.

I lay down on my bed, reached for my torch and shone it up at my clock. I waited for the second hand to sweep round, but it didn't move. I shone my torch at Jack's wall: his hour hand was on the 6, the minute hand was on the 12 and the second hand was stopped halfway between the 8 and the 9, just like mine. Jack sat up in his bed. I turned my torch towards him and he put his hands over his eyes.

'What are you doing?' he whispered.

'Something's wrong,' I said.

I stood up on my bed, reached out and tried to push the second hand. 'They've stopped. The Russians have stopped the clocks.'

Jack's face shone white in the dark except for the hole where his mouth hung open. He reached under his bed for his torch and fumbled for the switch. The beam lit our clocks and our posters, the undercarriage of our planes and turned them into huge shadows on the ceiling.

'He can't be gone,' he said. 'Dad can't be gone . . . It's still T minus—'

His torchlight stopped on my easel in the corner. The last number I'd written was 1, but now it was crossed through and underneath was a circle with a line scratched through it. I walked over and put my hand on the board. It wasn't my zero, I didn't do my zeros like that.

Jack stood beside me. His breaths were quick and heavy. I put my arm around him and looked at the white on my finger.

'What's that?' he asked.

I showed him the chalk. He shook his head and pointed to an envelope jammed between the hinges of the easel:

Special Delivery for Jack and Tom Gagarin.

I reached up and pulled the envelope out. My heart was thudding, my hands were shaking. Dad's writing wobbled in front of me and started to turn blurry. I didn't want to open it, I didn't want him to have gone, because if I'd known it was T minus zero I wouldn't have waved from the window, I would have run across the path and said goodbye properly.

Jack nudged me, told me to open the letter.

I slid my finger under the envelope.

Dear Jack, Dear Tom.
    Gone to the moon.
    Back soon.
    Love, Dad

I thought about Dad and the things we had talked about when we were lying on the grass, looking up at the stars. I knew he'd said he'd send a letter but this wasn't from the moon, and I thought he would have written more, not just told us he was going.

I felt cold. I felt sick. I looked at Jack, he was biting on his bottom lip and there were tears shining on his face. I put the letter back in the envelope and we walked downstairs to find Mum.

The front door was wide open. The wind blew through the hall. I called for Mum. She didn't answer. Jack closed the door and we walked towards the kitchen. There were no lights to guide us, just the red glow of the cooker switch on the wall.

I wanted to find Mum, I wanted to show her the letter, but the further I went down the hall, the slower I walked, until I was creeping like I was searching for ghosts. Jack slipped his hand in mine. I called for Mum again.

I heard a sniff.

We walked into the kitchen, looked into the dining room, then towards the back door. Mum was sitting on the back step looking out into the garden.

'Mum,' I said.

She turned around and smiled, then slid along the step and made space for us. I sat down beside her. The cold of the concrete made my feet ache. I handed her the letter, asked her if she wanted to read it, but from the look on her face I could tell she already knew what it said.

She put her arms around me and Jack and we sat on the step in silence, listening to the distant hum of the milk float and the rattle of bottles, and a tweet from the first bird in the sky. We looked down over the garden, over the electricity station, towards the dim lights of the building on the side of the hill. I imagined Dad inside, wired up to the monitors, with his heart beating mountains and valleys in a jagged green line.

Our dad going to the moon was supposed to be more exciting than this. People were supposed to be cheering, people were supposed to be waving. He was supposed to walk out of the cosmodrome, stop in front of flashing cameras and have his picture taken on a metal gantry. He was supposed to go to the moon in a blast of smoke and flames, not sitting in the back of a yellow taxi.

The clouds moved apart and the sky got brighter. Then the street lights turned off one by one.

Chapter Twelve

We've fallen off the table onto the floor. Our head aches and our arm hurts. We crawl out the door and lie on the platform with our head against the wall. The sky is blue and our breath smokes in the air.

A pigeon hoots.

We cup our hands over our mouth and hoot twice.

The pigeon hoots back.

We laugh.

We're happy.

Because the sun is shining.

Because the smell of liver isn't choking our throats.

We step down the stairs and turn underneath. We find a door in the shadow, push it open and walk inside. It's dark and stinks of piss.

And wee.

It's the same thing.

Oh.

We flick a light switch and sit down on the toilet. The door swings open, we jam it closed with our foot because, even though we can't hear anyone coming, we never know if someone will.

Like George Hart.

—

We don't like George Hart.
Can we just go to the toilet?
George Hart is fat.
George Hart was a fat bastard.
!

—

He wanted our sweets.
He wanted our money. He turned us upside down
and stuffed our head in the toilet.
It fell out of our pockets.
I told you to put it in our shoes.

—

—

. . . *There's a paper.*
What?
On the floor. Can we read it?
No . . . I don't think we should.
Why not?
Because papers only have bad news.
But this one might be different.
It won't be.
We reach down by the side of the toilet and pick up
the newspaper.
I said—
Uh-oh!
What?

It looks just like Frost.

Shit!

But he's got curly hair.

Fuck!

Boy dies in . . . What does that say?

Jesus—

Does it?

We throw the newspaper on the floor. It was bad enough knowing Frost was dead in our head, it looks even worse in black and white.

Tom? Tom?

What? What?

We look down at the paper.

There's a picture of you.

There's a picture of us.

!

We need to get out of here.

But what about our story? I've been practising my words.

They won't believe us.

We open the door.

Aren't we going to wash?

No.

But Mum said—

We take our T-shirt off and turn on the taps. Our blood swirls around the sink and drains down the plug. We feel hot and sick.

Because of the blood.

Because of Fr—

The sink starts to flicker and everything around it turns black like we are going into a tunnel. We splash water over our face, it drips down our neck, onto our chest and makes us shiver. Our legs shake. We hold onto the sink, lift our head to get air and see our face split in a cracked mirror.

Boo!

I wish you wouldn't do that.

We sway towards the mirror. Our face gets bigger, our face gets smaller.

We've got eyes like a monster.

And a nose like Pinocchio . . . but we don't tell lies.

No.

We never tell lies.

—

We never tell lies.

Jack!

Sorry.

We press our hands on the sides of our head.

To push ourself back together?

To take away the pain.

Dr Smith said we had to take deep breaths.

I am . . . We are.

Our arms shake, our sweat turns cold. We put our head against the mirror.

Are we going to take our pills?

No!

?

We'll never take the pills.

—

—

We stand up, put on our T-shirt and turn to go outside for air.

Wait!

What?

We look in the mirror. Our T-shirt is on back-to-front. There are blackberry bullet holes splattered across our back like we have been shot while running away.

But we haven't.

We might be now.

We hear the sound of an engine and the rumble of music. We go to the doorway and look out. A car door slams shut on the other side of the fence.

Our planes!

Our book!

We run up the stairs, back into the office and find our bag on the table. Outside a woman with black hair steps through the gate in the fence carrying a cardboard box under her arm. She walks across the yard, puts the box down on the bottom step and disappears towards the toilets.

We creep down the stairs, but the slower we go, the more they rattle. We take two steps at a time, jump the last four, then run across the yard between the lorries.

This one?

We run past numbers 6 and 5.

I thought you were good with numbers?

I am.

We pull back the canopy and climb into number 9.

Car engines rumble, then stop. Doors open and shut. We peer out through a gap in the canopy and watch two men stand and talk.

'I got the Blackpool run.'

'Say hello to Fiona for me.'

'Ha! I will.'

They laugh.

One of the men walks towards us. We back away from the gap.

Keys jangle. The gates creak open. A woman screams.

'Blood! Blood!'

Oh no.

Oh shit!

'What!'

'Blood! Everywhere!'

'Calm down, Beryl.'

'Call the police!'

Don't call the police.

Please don't call the police.

We move across the trailer and look out through a small hole in the canopy. The men run across the yard. Beryl comes out of the office with her hands over her eyes.

'And in there too, all over my typewriter.'

One man puts his arm around her, the other goes inside.

'Is there anything missing?'

Only biscuits.

——

. . . *And batteries.*

Shush!

. . . *And a big map of Great Britain.*

'I don't know . . . I can't tell.'

'Must be an animal . . . a fox . . . a badger.'

'An animal that smashes glass?' asks Beryl.

'Or an animal that types?' A man walks out onto the platform holding a piece of paper.

Jack, you didn't.

——

'Dear Beryl.' The man laughs. 'Dear Beryl. Sorry we smashed the glass, sorry we ate your biscuits . . .'

You idiot!

I couldn't help it.

How did you know her name was Beryl?

It was written on the stapler.

!

'Sorry about the blood . . . we didn't mean to do it.'

!

——

Well, at least you didn't—

'Now we're going to the beach. Love Jack and Tom.'

Shit!

The men laugh and walk across the yard. Beryl shakes her head and goes inside.

We take our eye away from the hole. We think about our picture in the paper. We think about the police, how they will know where we have been and where we are going, how they will get the dogs to follow the trail of our blood across the yard.

Will they?

They might. But we can't wait for them to come looking.

We hear footsteps outside our trailer. A man starts to whistle as the lorry door clicks open and the engine begins to rumble. We hold onto the sides of the trailer to stop ourself falling over. The engine gets louder, a horn blasts like a lighthouse in the fog.

'Tell Beryl it was just kids.'

'I will.'

The lorry pulls away. We grip the sides tighter but our trailer doesn't move.

!

!

We look out through the gap.

Jack.

What?

The trailer wasn't attached.

!

We jump down onto the tarmac and run after the lorry. Horns blast as two more lorries loom up behind us and overtake. We run between them towards the gates, through a cloud of blue fumes that smoke from the exhausts. We put our hand over our nose and mouth and hold our breath but the fumes sting our eyes and creep through our fingers.

We cry.

We cough.

We stagger through the gates out onto the road. Lorries, cars and buses roar around us as we run along-side the fence.

I'm sorry.

Not now.

I'm sorry I wrote—

I said—

A police car speeds towards us, overtakes a bus, then a lorry.

We stop running.

Because we're tired.

Because we'll look suspicious.

We walk quickly. The police car flashes by. We look over our shoulder and watch as it goes past the depot and disappears into a line of traffic in the distance.

Are we safe?

Yes. I think so.

We walk along a road that is wide and dusty where the chimneys of red factories stretch up into the sky. The further we walk, the smaller the buildings get, until they turn into warehouses and big open spaces filled with cars. We keep walking, wait for the road to turn west. That's what Dad told us: always go west; the same way he told us that hitch-hikers might get their hands ripped off if they hold out their arms and stick out their thumbs!

Ooops!

!

——

I'm sorry.

——

I'm sorry I wrote the letter.

It's OK. Forget it.

Oh good. So it's OK we took the rubber as well?

!

Summer 1971

All the days had disappeared and the last hour had passed. The sun was shining in through the sitting-room window and me and Jack were sitting on the settee eating breakfast while we watched TV. I heard the crackle of a man talking on a radio. It was T minus six minutes, fifty-three seconds and counting.

I heard a noise, a beep, beep, glitsch, then a voice crackled on a radio. It was talking backwards like Dad when he started to learn Russian.

I saw a picture, a rocket on a launch pad lit up bright in the dark. Clouds of smoke poured out the bottom and swirled around the letters written on the side. There was a clock in the corner of the screen, not like the ones Dad had made for us – it was just a series of flickering numbers that seemed to make time go twice as fast.

Jack got up, went over to the window and looked up at our hill.

'Why can't I see the rocket?' he asked.

It was because the Russians had changed the launch site.
Yes.
Because there were too many shepherds.

No.

Because there were too many—

It was because of the weather.

Oh.

I heard a whooshing noise on the TV, then a voice.

'10 – 9 – 8 – 7 – Sporry-wurry-sputnik. Beep.'

Jack sat down by my side. 'Was that Dad talking?'

I didn't know and I was too busy watching and listening to think of an answer.

'6 – 5 – 4 –'

Flames shot out the bottom of the rocket, smoke spiralled out and made the letters on the side of the rocket disappear. Jack squeezed my arm.

'Is it going to catch fire?' he asked.

'It's not real smoke,' I said. 'It's liquid nitrogen, it cools the rocket down.' But I don't think he believed me, because his eyes opened wider as the flames grew bigger and the numbers on the clock jumped up and down in the corner of the TV.

'3 – 2 – 1 – 0.'

The flames turned from orange to blue, but the rocket stayed still. Some strange writing flashed up on the screen:

МЫ ИМЕЕМ ПОДНЯТЬ – МЫ ИМЕЕМ СТАРТ

Lift-off! We have lift off!

Shush!

But that's what it said.
We didn't know that then.

The flames got higher, the smoke got thicker, but the rocket looked like it was stuck. Me and Jack looked at each other. For something that could travel at 17,000 miles per hour it seemed to be taking a long time to take off.

The launch pad fell away and disappeared into the dark. The rocket started to rock, then slowly it lifted off the ground. People began to cheer and clap inside the TV. Me and Jack did the same in our sitting room.

'Sporry-wurry-sputnik. Beep – beep – glitschhhhh!'

The rocket went high, disappeared into the clouds, then came out the other side. We watched it climb with smoke trailing behind it.

There was a big flash. A piece of metal broke off the rocket and fell from the sky. Jack thought the rocket had exploded. I told him it was the boosters, that they have parachutes so they fall gently back to Earth, then the Russians can use them again.

I looked back at the TV but all I could see was blue sky.

No one was clapping.

No one was talking.

The picture shook and went blurred. The camera searched for the rocket but all it could find were the smoke trails that had been left behind.

The picture changed to a newsreader sitting behind a desk. He said that communication with Soyuz 11 had been lost because they had gone behind the moon and that it would be two hours before they came round again. Then the screen went blank.

I walked over to the window. The sun was shining on our hill, the grass had turned from green to brown. I wondered if Dad had taken his samples with him or if he'd left them at the top in the freezer. I looked at Jack, at the blank TV, then at the clock. If we hurried we had time to climb our hill and check before the Russians came around again.

We were hot when we got to the top. The wind blew and stuck our T-shirts to our bodies. We took them off and walked under our swing poles, between the fridge and the washing machine. I told Jack to look for scorch marks while I looked for pools of nitrogen. We knew Dad had launched from somewhere else but we thought he might have had a practice run before he went. But by the time we'd walked a circle of the launch site, I realised that nothing had changed.

We walked between the wheels and the tyres and stopped by the freezer in the middle. The top had turned yellow from the sun, the sides had turned brown from the rain. I picked up the combination lock, turned the cog and entered the number 090334, the birth date of Yuri Gagarin. I threaded the lock through the handle and lifted the lid. My blood bumped through my palms. I looked inside. All Dad's samples had gone. All that was left was hundreds of yellow bags. I threaded the lock back through the handle and shut the lid, and as we walked back across our hill I wondered if the rocket would take longer to go around the moon now that Dad's samples were weighing it down.

I checked my watch when we got to the edge of the hill. There were only twenty minutes left. Me and Jack started our engines and flew all the way home.

We ran—

Can I do this bit?
?
Can I do the next bit?
It's important.
I know.
So you have to get it right.
I will.
OK.
. . . *What if I get stuck?*
Then I'll help.

——

——

——

Hu-hum.
!
Ready?

Yes.

We ran into the sitting room. Tom turned the telly on and we waited for the picture. It took ages, all I could see were dark shadows. The picture got brighter. Tom nudged me. Three astronauts wearing funny hats were floating around inside our TV.

Cosmonauts.

Isn't it the same?

No, cosmonauts are from Russia.

. . . And astronauts are from America?

Yes.

Two of the cosmonauts waved, the other one flicked switches. I think that was Dad. I knocked on the screen but he wouldn't turn round. Tom said I should leave him alone because he looked busy. The other two floated towards me. I asked Tom how they floated. He said it was . . .

Gravity . . . It's what keeps our feet on the ground.

I know.

—

. . . The telly made that funny sound. Beep, beep, glitschhhh! One of the cosmonauts unwrapped a piece of chocolate, let it float in the air, then swam after it like a fish. Dad kept flicking switches. The other cosmonaut laughed, so did me and Tom. We always laugh at the same things.

Yes.

Because we're twins?

Not that again.

But we used to wear the same clothes.

Only when I'd grown out of mine.

People used to say I was like you.

You were. You are . . . I think you should get on with the story.

. . . The cosmonaut opened his mouth wide and swallowed the piece of chocolate. I wondered how they breathed. Tom said it was oxygen, that they stored it in tanks. I was worried it might run out. Tom said it wouldn't.

Nothing happened for a while so I went to get a drink. I took big slow steps to the door with my arms out wide. 'Look, Tom,' I said. 'I'm floating.' He laughed and got up and did the same.

You're getting good at this.

Thanks . . . The telly made that beeping noise again. Beep, beep. Glitch! And a cosmonaut did a somersault and ate a piece of jelly . . . What was the beeping noise again?

The radio . . . the Russians' radio . . . it beeped when they finished talking.

But why? Beep.

Have we got to do this again?

Yes. Beep.

!

So why did their radio beep? Beep.

So they didn't all talk at the same time. Beep.

Like us?

——

Like us?

——

Why won't you answer?

Because you didn't say beep. Beep.

Aaaargh!

Ha!

You do that every time. Beep.

I think we should stop now.

Because you're bored?

Because we've got a headache.

. . . *Sorry.*

———

Sorry. Beep.

It's OK.

———

It's OK. Beep.

. . . *I think you're better at telling the story. Beep.*

———

———

The cosmonauts floated around inside our TV for the rest of the afternoon. Me and Jack took it in turns going to the kitchen or the toilet so we could tell each other what had happened. The Russians floated and did experiments while Dad flicked switches and wrote things down. I told Jack about the satellites, how they sent pictures back to Earth, and I told him about the first rockets, that they used to send monkeys but they pushed the wrong button and blew up.

I feel sorry for the monkeys.

?

I feel sorry for the monkeys.

It's OK. They don't go any more.

Why not?

Because they sent Yuri Gagarin instead.

Our dad?

I said Yuri, not Steve.

Our uncle then?

No.

But Dad said Yuri was his brother.

He said he was his comrade.

Is that the same thing?

No . . . yes . . . you're confusing me.

Me too.

All I know is that Yuri is in Russia behind the Iron Curtain.

?

It's a curtain wrapped all around Russia so that people can't get in or out.

Can't they pull it back?

No.

Because it's too heavy?

Because they don't want to.

But Dad's stuck behind it with Yuri?

I don't think so.

And Yuri is our uncle?

!

?

He can't be.

Why not?
Because we used to be Kings.

——

——

The next morning me and Jack got up early and ate our cereal while the Russians ate pills and sucked water through straws. It was Sunday and the sun was shining. We thought about going out and playing football. We thought about climbing our hill, but even though we'd only seen the back of Dad's head we couldn't risk going out in case he turned round.

We listened to him talk on his radio and tried to work out what he was saying, but the radio crackled all the time and when it didn't crackle it beeped. We thought maybe it was a message, like Morse code, or a secret language like the Americans used when they were on the moon.

A small step for a giant?

——

A giant step for an astronaut.
You've got it wrong again.
But it was something like that?
Yes . . . it was something like that.

At dinner time we ate shepherd's pie. The Russians ate space dust wrapped up in silver foil. Me and Jack stuck magnets to our trays to stop our knives and forks from floating around. They screwed up the foil and put it in compartments. Jack wondered why they didn't throw it outside. I told him if they opened the door they would get sucked away, that they had waste dumps for rubbish and flue dumps for their toilet, and he laughed when I told him the cosmonauts couldn't burp in space.

We watched the Russians all afternoon until the picture started to fade and the TV smelt like it was burning. Mum came in three times, said it was really hot outside and that me and Jack should go out and play. I pretended not to hear. Jack turned the sound down. Mum went back out and I closed the curtains to block out the sun.

The Russians had gone when she came in the fourth time. Jack was asleep on the settee and I was watching a man show another man how to make a pot on a wheel. Mum sat down beside me.

'What happened to the rocket?' she asked.

'No reception,' I said.

'Is it the aerial?'

'No,' I said. 'They've gone behind the moon again.'

She put her arm around me and we watched another man try to make a pot. We thought it was good until the wheel went too fast and the clay got too high, and we laughed when it collapsed and he had to start again.

I told her about the Russians, how Dad had been pressing buttons and hadn't turned around all day.

'Maybe he was writing a letter,' she said.

I asked her if he was going to write one for her too.

'I hope so.' She smiled and looked sad at the same time.

The meter clicked under the stairs, the lights went out, the TV flickered bright, then off. Everything was quiet except for the sound of a car droning up the hill and Jack snoring. I waited for Mum to get up but she didn't move.

'Is the money on the shelf?' I whispered.

'There's none left,' she said. 'I'll borrow some from Auntie Jean in the morning.'

She went into the hall and found some candles in the cupboard under the stairs and lit them in front of the fire.

I looked out the window, saw the orange of the street light shine through the curtain. Mum sat beside me. I told her I was sorry there was no electricity left for her to watch her programme. She smiled, said she was tired and that it had been a long day. I told her it had been long and exciting, that it would get even better when Dad sent me a letter.

I asked her how he would post it and how long it would take to get here. She squeezed me tight and whispered like she was saying her prayers. I told her I couldn't hear. She said it didn't matter, that she was talking to herself, then she pulled me back with her on the settee and we watched the little dot in the middle of the TV glow white and disappear.

Chapter Thirteen

We reach a village with tiny houses—
And a church.

And a monument with a cross, with a circle of poppies around the bottom that have been turned grey by the sun and the rain.

We sit down on a step, rest our back against a wall and look up. A church tower sticks out of the ground with a clock at the top. One hand points at the eleven, the other points at the twelve. The wind blows through a tree and somewhere a bird sings. We rest our head against the wall and feel our heart beat slowly against the stone. A road winds away from us between the houses and gets smaller and smaller until it twists around a corner and disappears. There are no lorries driving at us, there are no cars flashing by. There is no one shouting out of windows, there is no one slamming doors.

—

—

—

It's like everyone has gone to the moon.
It's like everyone died in the war.

—

—

—

—

We look back at the cross and see the names of people who died in the First and Second World Wars.

George Barclay.

Dennis Foot. VC.

Cyril Arkwright. DSO.

Kenneth Abbot. DCM.

Names we have never heard of and letters of the medals they won—

Victoria Cross, Distinguished Service Order, Distinguished Conduct Medal.

We think of Dad and the shiny medals that were pinned on his uniform and we remember the day when Mum helped us make medals of our own. She found some old coins in a tin. We wrapped them in foil and rubbed them with our fingers until the Queen's head shone through. Mum tied them with red ribbon and we hung them around our necks. She said we looked smart, that Dad would like them. The next day she drove us to watch Dad in the homecoming parade.

It was raining, people were stood on the edge of the square hiding under their umbrellas. A sergeant was shouting orders, his voice echoed off buildings while the regiment marched up and down in green uniforms with berets on their heads. We wanted them to stop.

We wanted to find Dad but their arms and legs moved so fast they were all blurred.

The sergeant kept shouting and the soldiers kept marching, suddenly the whistle sounded and they all stood still.

I ducked under the rope.

I followed and we ran across the square.

My heart started bumping.

My head was thudding. It was like we were lost in the supermarket and didn't know the way home. Dad shouted. We turned around. He was stood there smiling with his arms open wide holding his beret in his hand. We ran towards him. He wrapped his arms around us and wouldn't let go. We showed him our medals and he said they were as bright and heavy as his. We told him we were glad he was back and couldn't wait to show him all our new planes and rockets when we got home. He rubbed our heads and hugged Mum. We thought he was home to stay.

We didn't know it was only for two weeks.

We thought that he'd finished fighting. We didn't know the war was still going on.

———

———

A bell rings and makes us jump. We look up at the church clock and see the two hands pointing at the sky.

———

———

What do we do now?

—

What do we do now? Beep.
We're thinking.
Still?

—

—

We should have known that running away would be hard, that escaping was the easy part. But we don't have to keep running so fast. Just because Dad travelled faster than sound doesn't mean we have to do the same. Mum used to say that when we got stuck writing our book, she used to say that good things—
Come in little packages?
!
Like me.
Mum used to say that good things will come to those who wait.
Oh.

—

We tap our trainers on the step.

—

So are we just going to stay here?
Yes. Sometimes the best way to hide is to stay still.
That's what we told James Lewis.
I know.
And it didn't work.

It wasn't our fault.

?

It was his idea to hide in the freezer.

——

——

We take the map from our bag and spread it out on the ground. It's torn and crumpled at the edges and where the cities and ports used to be there are big holes.

I thought I told you to take the pins out.

I forgot.

!

——

The roads and railway lines spread out like veins across the map. We wish there were more roads to choose from, more places to get lost in, but all we can see between us and Swansea is a place called Shrewsbury and lots of hills.

And we've got to climb them all.

——

An engine rattles between the houses.

We look up and see a yellow camper van come around the corner. We pick up our bag.

Run!

I thought you said to stay still.

In the church.

——

Behind the cross!

The camper van gets closer.

OK.

Forget it.

?

It's too late.

—

The camper van begins to slow and stops by the shop. We turn back to the monument, read the names on the cross.

George Barclay. Dennis Foot . . . We've already read this.

Pretend.

—

The van door creaks open. We sneak a look over our shoulder and see a girl get out.

She's wearing black boots with flowers on the toes.

She's got a red ribbon in her hair.

She looks across at us, grins like she is excited then lifts her hand like she's going to wave.

Don't!

Too late.

We lift our hand and wave back.

!

The girl smiles, runs with little steps and goes inside the shop.

I thought I told you not to?

But she looked nice.

—

She looked nice. Beep.

I know.

We put our head down and stare at the hole where London used to be.

Can we talk to her?

No.

Because of me?

Because of us.

So can't we talk to anyone?

Not really.

What about if I was quiet? I could be quiet.

You couldn't do it for Dr Smith.

——

——

I could whisper.

People will still hear you.

Not if I do it like this.

No, they'll still hear.

How about this then?

——

Hello. Hello.

Actually, that works.

Oh good.

We look across at the shop. The girl is so small that we can only just see the top of her head as she walks up and down the aisle. Our heart begins to thud. Her head turns from side to side then moves up and down as she stops to talk to the man behind the counter. She points out the window. We look down at our map.

Is she talking about us?

——

Does she know?

Why are we whispering now?

I'm practising.

!

So does she know?

No one knows about us.

Except Dr Smith.

——

. . . Mrs Unster . . . and Frost.

Shush!

The man walks out from behind the counter, picks up a loaf of bread and puts it in a bag. The girl stands beside him and smiles at us. We feel a weird tingle inside, between our stomach and our heart. It's a long time since we have seen a girl. It's been even longer since we have seen a girl smile.

Clare Macfarlane.

Yes.

We liked Clare Macfarlane. She liked us.

She liked me . . . until you cut holes in her curtains.

She said she couldn't see the stars.

——

Why did you touch—

That was her fault.

So why's it always us that has to run away?

Because...

Because?

Shit!

What?

We look down at our clothes, at the mud on our trainers and trousers, at the blood and blackberry stains on our shirt.

We need to cover this up.

——

We untie our jumper from our waist and pull it over our head. The shop bell rings. We push our head through the hole and pull our sleeve over the cut on our hand. The girl walks out of the shop, her eyes dart up and down the road like she's waiting for traffic. Our map flaps in the wind. We pick up a stone, put it on a corner and pretend to follow the road from Glasgow to Inverness.

We hear the sound of boots taking little steps as she hurries across the road.

She's coming.

I know. Remember, don't talk to her.

I won't.

The steps stop. We look over the edge of the map, see the girl's boots standing at the bottom. We hear a click and the hiss of air. We look up and watch her drink from a can in the shadow of the cross.

Hello.

I give up.

The girl takes the can down from her lips. Her eyes sparkle with water.

'Hello.' She nods at our map. 'Are you going far?'

Two hundred and thirty six thousand, one hundred and twenty miles!

!

The girl laughs.

Our skin goes hot. Our face starts to throb.

I told you not to.

Sorry.

I'll walk away.

No, I'll stop.

Promise?

Promise.

The girl's shadow creeps across the map.

'No, really,' she says. 'How far are you going?'

___

?

'Ooops, is it a secret?' She puts her hand up to her mouth.

Go on.

What?

Talk to her.

'Well?'

No, it's not a secret.

We point to the hole above Port Talbot.

'That's a long way to go for a hole,' she laughs.

A vein throbs in our neck, we feel our face turning red. We look down the road. A postman pushes his bike and leans it against a lamp post. He pushes open

228

a gate, goes up a path and delivers a letter. We wish she would talk again, we wish she would sit down beside us, we wish she would do anything just to fill the silence.

—

—

She sits down on the step and puts her bag between us.

We smell bread—

We smell violets.

The girl pulls a loaf of bread out of her bag.

The postman wheels his bike to the next house.

'Want some?'

She breaks off a piece of bread and taps us on the arm.

'Do you want some?'

Yes please.

We take the bread, rip a piece off and shove it in our mouth.

Chew slower.

We're hungry.

The girl laughs. We chew for a minute and try to think of something to say.

What's your name? Where are you from? How old are you? When's your birthday?

I know. I know.

'Sorry?' She puts her head on the side like she's heard a whisper from the cross.

We choke. Bits of bread fall out the side of our mouth.
'Are you OK?'

Yes. Sorry. It's been a long time since—

We sat next to a girl.

Since I ate.

She grins and shrugs at the same time.

'Here,' she says.

We take the can in our good hand and drink. The
coke is so cold and fizzy that it stings our throat and—

Ice cream headache! Ice cream headache!

!

The girl laughs. 'Do a handstand,' she says.

Can we?

No.

We hold our head and squeeze tight until the pain
starts to fade. Out the corner of our eye we can see the
girl looking at us. An ache starts to grow inside, in our
stomach, up to our chest. All the things we want to say
tumble around in our head. What's your name? Where
are you from? How old are you? When's your birthday?
They go round and round and all the time we are thinking
we can see her out the corner of our eye waiting for
one of our thoughts to come out. She tilts her head back
and looks at the sky. The sun shines on her face, turns
her skin white, turns the ends of her hair red. We look
up and see a white cloud float across the sky.

Can't you think of anything?

!

It's a cumulonimbus.

That's a good one!

'Sorry?'

The cloud . . . it's a cumulonimbus.

'Oh, that's nice.'

A trickle of sweat runs down our back. We pull at the neck of our jumper to try and get some air. She watches us. We look down at our jumper, at the yellow line knitted across the brown.

'You look like a bee,' the girl says. 'Or Captain Hook.'

He was a pirate!

Shit!

We put our hand over our mouth.

Sorry, forgot.

The girl puts her hand on our knee. 'It's OK,' she says. 'I've got a friend that stutters.'

Oh that's handy.

We smile, look at the ground and try to think of the next word that we might get stuck on.

———

Where are you from? How old are you? When's your birthday?

I'm trying.

'How did you do it?'

?

?

We look up. She nods at our hand.

Uh oh!

———

We slide our sleeve down.

———

We— I was mugged . . . two days ago.

!

She screws up her face as she looks at the jagged line across our knuckles and the dried blood trapped under our nails.

'It looks quite nasty,' she says. 'Was it glass? It can be bad if it's glass.' She looks at us like she cares. We look at the ground again. We have already told her one lie; she seems too nice for us to tell another.

He—

He had a knife.

!

'Oh no, did you call the police?'

No, we never call the police.

No . . . he would have been gone before they got there.

She looks across the road, bites her bottom lip like she's thinking.

'One minute,' she says. 'Wait here.'

She jumps up and runs back across the road. We watch her hair bob up and down and her dress blow in the wind. She slides back the door on her van and climbs in.

Can we talk properly now?

Yes.

Why did we lie?

—

Why did we lie?

Because she wouldn't like us if she knew the truth.

Can we talk to her more?

I'm trying.

But you're not very good.

—

—

—

Can I try?

No, it's better if you whisper.

I like whispering . . . I wish we'd thought of it before.

Me too.

The girl steps out of the van with a first aid box in one hand and a bowl in the other. She smiles as she walks back towards us.

'My name's Harriet by the way.'

Ha!

!

'And...'

?

!

'What's yours?'

Ja—

You dare.

Ha!

Tom.

She puts the bowl on the step and kneels in front of us. 'Well Tom,' she says. 'I think this will help.'

We rest our elbow on our knee. She holds our hand, puts her fingers underneath, rests them gently against ours.

Will it hurt?

No.

'It's OK,' she says. 'I'll be careful.' Her voice is suddenly quiet and soft as she reaches down, dips cotton wool into the bowl and drips water over our cut.

Our knuckles start to sting and our fingers start to tingle. Harriet gets another piece of cotton and reaches down for more water. A gold necklace hangs from her neck. We watch it swing from her chin to her chest.

She dabs the cotton wool gently around the cut. 'There,' she says. 'It's looking better already.'

Bloodied water drips off our hand and stains the stone. Harriet reaches back into the box and unravels a bandage. We anchor one end with our finger while she wraps the rest around our hand. Her breath is quiet and warm in our ear. We lean forward and watch her chest move up and down in the shade of her dress.

I don't think we—

'It's not too tight is it?'

We wriggle our fingers.

A little bit.

No, it's fine.

She smiles. A warm feeling goes through our body.

——

——

She tips the water out of the bowl and stands up.

Is she leaving?

I think so.

But she could give us a lift. She could help us find Dad.

——

Say something.

?

Where are you from? How old are you?—

Harriet starts to turn away.

——

Where are you from? How old are you? When's your birthday?

!

We put our hand over our mouth.

Thanks.

That's OK.

Harriet turns around and laughs.

'Sounds like we're in the army.'

We smile.

She pulls a strand of her hair back behind her ear.

'Cambridge . . . Nineteen . . . August . . .' She blinks quickly like she's got something in her eye. 'What about you?'

Lots of—

Hartlepool. Eighteen. July—

Two days ago.

'Oh, that's bad luck.'

?

What is?

'Getting mugged on your birthday.'

She smiles and walks across the road.

The air grows cold as the sun disappears. The postman starts to run from one door to another. We look up at the church and see dark clouds creeping towards us. Harriet comes back, picks up her can and puts it in a bin by the church wall. A raindrop lands on our head, another flicks our ear. The wind blows around our head. We look down and watch as raindrops start to splatter across our map. Harriet walks towards her van.

We wonder where she's going.

If it's on the way to Swansea...

Maybe we could go too.

The rain comes down harder, seeps through the holes in our jumper onto our skin. We pick up our map, fold it over our head and peer out through the holes. Harriet laughs and climbs in behind the wheel. We want to stop her, we want to hitch a ride, but we can't talk. It's too risky to talk.

But we like her.

I know.

The van turns in a circle, stops in front of us. Harriet winds down the window.

'Are you mad?'

———

We pull the map off our head and blink in the rain.

——

!

. . . Where are you going? Is it near Swansea? Can we come too?

She giggles again.

'I like this game . . . Not telling you. Not telling you . . . And I'm thinking about it.'

We stand up. The rain comes down harder, flattens our hair, drips down our neck. We shiver, lift up our arm, push our fringe out of our eyes. Harriet bites her lip. She looked pretty in the sun, she looks even prettier through the rain. She smiles as she reaches across and opens the door.

We climb in, throw our map in the footwell and hold our bag on our lap. The van smells of Harriet and Harriet smells of—

Coconut?

Yes.

We run our hand through our hair.

She's looking at us.

———

She's looking at us. Beep.

———

Beep!

!

'Sorry?'

. . . I thought you were going to hit the postman.

Ha!

The postman waves as he crosses in front of us. Harriet slowly shakes her head.

'You're funny,' she says.

We smile.

I think she likes us.

I think she likes you.

Is that OK?

I'm not sure.

———

———

Harriet lets out the handbrake, presses the accelerator. The van rattles and judders as we pull away. We clutch our bag to our chest. The rain runs down the windscreen, it turns the road into a river and blurs all the houses. The wipers squeak backwards and forwards but we still can't see where we're going. Harriet looks in the footwell, lifts up the lid of a box between the seats.

We lean forward, pull the sleeve over our hand and wipe our breath from the screen.

'Thanks.'

That's OK.

That's OK.

She reaches down, changes gear and we drive off through the rain.

Summer 1971

The day after Dad went to the moon me and Jack got up early and waited for the postman, but all he brought was two brown envelopes and the *History of the Universe* magazine. I went into the sitting room and turned on the TV but the Russians weren't on. I changed channels and searched for them but all I could find was a man pointing a stick at some triangles on a blackboard with letters and numbers underneath.

Me and Jack got ready for school but all we could think about was the Russians and waiting for Dad's letter to come through the post.

In the first lesson I swapped chairs with Matthew Simmons and piled my books up high on my desk so I could hide behind them and look out the window. Mr Taylor talked about the clouds, how they were made of water sucked up from the ocean and how they got heavier and heavier until they crashed into mountains. A magpie landed on a telephone wire. Mr Taylor kept talking but I wasn't listening because I was watching a DC-9 cut a line across the sky. I imagined myself in it, that my pen was my joystick. I pulled it towards me, the nose rose up and I flew high up into the jet stream. I saw something shining, a piece of glitter falling through the sky. I increased the throttle, got closer and closer until I drew level and saw Viktor and Georgi smiling at me through the window and I saw Dad turn around, hold up his hand and wave—

'King!' I heard Mr Taylor shout.

'King!' he shouted again.

Matthew Simmons nudged me.

'Gagarin.'

I turned away from the window. Everyone in the class was laughing. Mr Taylor was standing with the blackboard rubber aimed at me.

'Sorry, sir,' I said.

My heart was beating. I could feel my face turning red.

'Ah! At last. Welcome back Gagarin.'

I rubbed my head and I wondered how he'd known I'd been away. He pointed at the blackboard, at the clouds he had drawn and the writing underneath.

'So, tell us,' he said. 'Which one is the biggest, cumulonimbus or stratus?'

I checked back out the window; the DC-9 had disappeared. A chair scraped on the floor and Mr Taylor walked between the desks towards me. I didn't know what to do, whether to sit still or run. Before I could decide he was already standing behind me.

'So, which is biggest?'

'I don't know,' I said.

He put his hand on my head. I felt his fingers dig deep into my skull as he turned my head away from the window.

'You won't find the answer in the sky . . . It's written on the board.'

I wanted to tell him about the Russians, that they were in space, that my dad was up there with them, that he was a cosmonaut and Mr Taylor must have seen them all on TV. But I remembered Dad's words, 'Tell no one, it's a secret.' So I said nothing. Mr Taylor let go of my head and said perhaps I'd like to tell him in detention instead.

At break time I walked around the edge of the playground, still looking at the sky. I got hit by the football and tripped by ropes. I stopped for a drink at the fountain and then I went round again. I heard girls screaming, I heard a boy shout, Watch out! My head banged against the netball post and I fell to the ground. My ears were ringing, my jaw was aching. I opened my eyes and saw the older kids circled around me like I'd been knocked down in a fight.

'What are you doing?' one said.

I rubbed my head.

'Looking for the Russians,' I said.

They looked at me like I was dumb.

At the end of the day I ran down the road and met Jack outside his school gates. His shoes were scuffed and his shirt was torn. He had a bandage on his elbow and a red blob of disinfectant on his knee.

'What happened?'

He screwed up his face like it still hurt.

'I fell over,' he said. 'I was looking at the sky.'

I took his bag and put it on my back and I laughed because
he had spent his day walking around the playground looking for
the Russians just like me.

We started to walk down the road. Jack dragged his feet. I
told him to go faster, that I wanted to get back and see if we
had a letter. We crossed the road on the corner by the church.
Jack opened his arms wide, I did the same, and we flew like
aeroplanes all the way home.

Our front door was open, like it had been all summer. We kicked
off our shoes and hung our bags on top of Dad's jacket in the
hall. Mum was in the sitting room talking to Auntie Jean. I asked
if we had a letter. Mum nodded at an envelope on top of the TV.

TOP-SECRET
FOR THE EYES OF JACK AND
TOM GAGARIN ONLY

I picked the letter up, tried to slip my finger under the flap,
but my hands were shaking too much to find a gap in the glue.

Mum held out her hand.

'Let me try,' she said.

'You can't,' I said. 'It's for our eyes only.'

She smiled. 'It's OK,' she said. 'I'm sure Dad won't mind.' She slid
her nail under the paper and gave it back to me.

The letter was creased in the middle and torn across the top. I knelt down, placed it on the floor and flattened it out like a map. Jack lay on his stomach beside me and together we read our first letter from the moon.

7th June 1971

Dear Jack, Dear Tom.

Yesterday we pointed the rocket at the stars. All the bones in my body got jumbled up. Georgi was sick, Viktor needed to pee. My tonsils wobbled in my throat. The sky went black, then blue. Ooops, I nearly forgot. Georgi and Viktor say Hi.

Hi!

Hi!

They are very funny and friendly. Did you see us all on TV?

I'm sorry if my letter took a long time. Georgi keeps missing the post and we have to wait twenty-four hours before it comes around again.

Georgi says sorry.

Sorry!

Viktor says Hi again.

Hi!

When they stop talking it is quiet here. I get tired and I've got blisters on my fingers.

Jack, I'm still looking for your monsters.

Tom, the Earth spins so fast it makes me dizzy. Look the speed up in your encyclopaedia.

Got to go, Viktor says I've got to push another button.

Will write soon.

Dad

X One for Tom   X One for Jack   X One for Mum

~~~~~~

I read the letter three times to Jack and another hundred in my head. I thought how happy he sounded, and I was glad that the Russians were his friends and now we knew their names. I ran my finger across the moon he had drawn and thought how no one else at school would have had a letter that came from so far away.

I folded it up and put it back in the envelope. Mum said I should keep it safe. I found our book and put it inside. Jack turned the TV on and he watched the Russians. I got my pen and tried to write a letter back to Dad. I told him what I'd been doing, that I'd seen the rocket take off and that I'd seen him inside, but when someone has done something so exciting in their life it seemed boring to tell him what I'd been doing in mine. Mum saw me chewing the top of my pen. She told me not to worry, that Dad would still love my letter no matter how much I wrote. I tried to write again but no more words came out, then Jack turned around, took the pen out of my hand and drew a picture that took up the rest of the page. I put the letter in an envelope and addressed it to Dad on the moon, then I put it on the mantelpiece and Mum said she would post it in the morning after me and Jack had gone to school.

That's what we did all that week: got up, waited for a letter, went to school, walked around in circles, flew home, found Mum was sometimes out, Auntie Jean was always in and she'd fall asleep while we watched the Russians on TV. And during that week I wrote to Dad every night and told him that Mr Taylor had talked about the altostratus and the cirrus and Jack told him that Mrs Gough had taught him to tell the time, that there were sixty seconds in a minute, sixty minutes in an hour and sixty hours in a day. I didn't tell Jack that he'd got the last bit wrong because it didn't matter that week – the only time that counted was the one on our clocks, and the only clouds that mattered were the ones that floated across the moon at night and got in the way.

As the days passed the Russians were on TV less and less, until for the last three days of the week they weren't on at all. The only picture of them we saw was one that flashed on the screen for five seconds at the end of the news. But me and Jack couldn't even watch that in peace, because every afternoon before tea Auntie Jean walked along the path and came into our house. Ever since Dad had gone to the moon it was like she had moved in. On the first day of the summer holidays she was round our house all day. Me and Jack were in the sitting room. He was building a rocket out of Lego, I was gluing stickers to the wings of my planes. Auntie Jean was talking to Mum in the kitchen.

'How long has it been now?'

'Nearly two weeks.'

'And they haven't been out since he's been gone?'

'No ... Only to school ... All they do is watch TV ...'

I put my stickers down and listened more closely.

'Their teachers are worried,' she said. 'Mr Taylor says Tom's not paying attention.'

'It's only to be expected.'

'I know, but they've even stopped talking to their friends . . . I wish—'

I heard a crash and looked over at Jack.

'I pressed too hard.' He pointed at his rocket that was now scattered into a hundred pieces on the floor. 'I'll make—'

I told him to shush. I listened for Mum and Auntie Jean, but it had gone quiet in the kitchen.

'What was that noise?' asked Mum.

I looked up. She was stood with Auntie Jean in the doorway. Jack pointed at the bricks.

'My rocket crashed.'

Mum and Auntie Jean smiled. I shuffled along the settee and they sat down beside me. Mum's face was red and blotchy. Her hair was tied back behind her head and her eyes were sparkling like she had been crying. Mum had been looking more and more tired each day. It was like she hadn't slept since Dad had gone.

'Mum,' I said, 'are you OK?'

She nodded quickly.

'It's only hay fever,' she said. She put her hand on my shoulder and nodded at my stickers and planes. 'You should finish those before the glue dries up.'

I dabbed the glue on a sticker and tried to stick it on a Spitfire but the glue stuck to my fingers and the wings tilted over. I tried again but there was more glue on the table than there was on my planes. I couldn't stop thinking about Mum and what she'd said in the kitchen and I wondered if she was wishing for the same thing as me, because after T plus fourteen days, twenty-two hours, fifteen minutes, twenty-three seconds and counting, I was wishing that Dad would come home.

We sat on the settee all afternoon with the TV flickering silently in the corner until Mum turned it up when the news came on. I looked at the screen. People wearing scarves and balaclavas ran through the streets in the rain. They stuffed rags in the tops of bottles, lit them with matches and threw them at the soldiers. The soldiers ran for cover, hid behind barricades as the bottles hit the road and burst into flames.

Out the corner of my eye I saw Auntie Jean slide her hand along the settee and put it on top of Mum's.

'It's OK, Miriam,' she whispered. 'At least he's safe now.'

I wondered what Auntie Jean meant, I wondered what she knew, but I didn't have time to ask as Jack was nudging me in my side because the Russians were back on.

I slid off the settee and knelt closer to the TV but all I saw was Georgi and Victor frozen in mid-air and Dad dead-still with his finger poised over a button. The newsreader said that no one had been in space for as long as the cosmonauts but he didn't know when they would be coming back down. I waited for him to say more. I waited for more pictures, but after less than ten seconds the Russians had gone. It was like they didn't matter any more. Everyone had been excited when they took off but now they were floating around in space nobody seemed to care. I looked at Mum.

'I want to see Dad,' I said.

'I know.'

'He's been up there for days and all I've seen is the back of his head.'

She held my hand.

'Maybe he'll be back on tomorrow,' she said.

But I was fed up with waiting, I was fed up with watching pictures of where Dad used to be, I wanted to see where he was now.

I stood up in the middle of the room. Auntie Jean leant round me. I turned and saw the weatherman on the TV.

'It's just the weather,' I shouted. 'It's not important, it's just hot and getting hotter. Go and buy your own telly. We want to watch the Russians. The Russians are important. Our dad is important.'

Auntie Jean put her hand over her mouth. Mum stared like she couldn't believe the words were coming out of me.

'T plus fourteen days, twenty-three hours, twenty-three minutes, forty-five seconds and counting ... That's how long he's been gone, that's how long we've been here watching.' My chest beat up and down, I tried to breathe deeper but the more I tried to speak, the more my words wouldn't come out. My throat started to ,throb, my eyes started to ache.

Mum stood up.

'It's OK,' she said. 'Everything will be OK.' She held out her arm, pulled me towards her and hugged me tight. I closed my eyes and started to cry. I felt her hand smooth my head. I thought about what I'd just said and felt bad inside. It wasn't her fault the Russians weren't on TV. It wasn't her fault everyone had forgotten them.

I heard a sniff. Auntie Jean wiped her nose with a tissue.

'I'm sorry,' I said.

'It's all right, Tom,' she said. She stood up and went out the door. I waited for Mum to tell me off but she just held me tighter. Auntie Jean shuffled along the path with her head pointed at the ground. I wished I hadn't shouted at her; she looked so old and lonely now she was walking on her own.

I didn't think I'd upset Auntie Jean very much though because she was around our house again the next day talking to Mum in the kitchen. Me and Jack were in the sitting room, but we didn't have to wait all day for the Russians to come on the news, because in the middle of the afternoon they were back on our TV. Viktor and Georgi were still floating, Dad was still flicking switches, but then the picture changed to a man with a beard wearing a baggy jumper.

He was a tramp.

He was a scientist.

He pointed at two circles on a blackboard and said one was the moon and one was the Earth. Then he drew an X in between them. He said the cosmonauts were in trouble, that he didn't really know what was happening because the Russians had stopped communication.

'What does that mean?' asked Jack.

'It means they're not talking.'

'To each other?'

'To us.'

We slid off the sofa and knelt in front of the TV.

The scientist pointed at the X, then drew a dotted line around the moon. He said the Russians would have to burn their engines to get out of the moon's orbit. He drew another dotted line from the rocket to the Earth. He said the next seventy-two hours were crucial, that he didn't know where or when the Russians would come back.

The picture switched back to the cosmonauts: Georgi opened his mouth and chased after food. Then the same picture played again. The scientist said it was a library picture, that even though the Russians still had communication with the cosmonauts they wouldn't let us see.

I went hot. Sweat trickled down my neck. I turned away from the TV and walked over to the window. Jack followed me.

The sun had gone down and our hill was a shadow. I looked up and wished I could see the Russians in the red sky. I wished Dad had taken a radio, I wished he'd turned around, I wished he'd written more in his letters. The first few days of him being in space had been exciting: watching him take off, watching Georgi eat, watching Viktor float. But now everything seemed to be going wrong.

I turned away from the window and went out into the kitchen. Mum was sat at the table with her head in her hands.

'Dad's in trouble,' I said.

Mum jumped.

'Have you . . .' She looked at Auntie Jean, then back at me. 'Have you been listening to us?'

'No,' I said. 'The scientist told us on the TV.'

I pulled the calendar off the fridge and gave it to Jack.

Mum stood up.

'What are you going to do?'

'We're going to work out when and where Dad is going to land.'

Me and Jack ran upstairs. I got my globe out of the cupboard and put it on the floor between our beds.

Jack slid his finger back to 6 June.

10.30. *Going to the moon.*

He walked his fingers along the days of the week. On every day Dad had drawn a question mark and at the bottom he'd scribbled, *Dad coming home.*

Jack looked up and asked what the question marks meant. I told him it was all the days Dad thought he might be coming home but he wasn't absolutely sure.

I turned the globe and followed the equator with my finger as it went over the Pacific, through Colombia and Brazil. Jack pointed.

'There!' he said. 'Dad could land there.'

I stopped the globe.

'The Democratic Republic of Congo?'

'Yes,' he said.

'No . . . I don't think Dad would land there.'

'Because it's too far away?'

'Because it's in the middle of the jungle.'

He shrugged, moved his finger further up the globe and landed on America. I shook my head and told him the Russians

253

wouldn't land there either because they weren't friends with the Americans.

But the Russians were our friends.
The ones in space were.

I turned the globe and we went from America, through Canada, jumped over the Atlantic Ocean, bounced on England, then on to France, Germany and Russia. There were so many oceans, there were so many countries, so many wide-open spaces where Dad could land. I held my hand in the air and imagined I was in Dad's rocket coming back to Earth.

Eeeeeeeeeeeoonnnnnnnnnngggggggg!
It didn't have propellers!
Oh.

I brought my hand closer, waited for the world to slow down and tried to find England again. But as I zoomed in, I thought that even if Dad had said he was going to land on our hill, if he was just one second late he'd end up in France.

The world stopped. I looked at Jack. I looked at Dad's writing and his question mark. If he couldn't work out when and where he was going to land, what chance did we have?

Mum was gone when we woke up the next morning. She'd left a note on the table for me and Jack to go to the shop and get some milk. We both wanted to stay in just in case the Russians came on TV, but Auntie Jean said that we should go out and that Mum had said we could spend the change.

We got our bikes out of the shed and cycled down the hill to the shop. Jack guarded our bikes while I went inside. Mr Marsh was standing behind the counter whistling while he stacked cigarette packets on a shelf. I put a bottle of Coke and a bottle of milk on the counter. He turned around and smiled when I gave him the money.

'How's your dad?' he asked.

'I don't know,' I said. 'The Russians have stopped talking.'

'The Russians?' he said.

I bit on my lip to stop any more words from getting out.

Mr Marsh shook his head, reached over the counter and gave me the change. I picked up the bottle and walked towards the door. I looked back, saw Mr Marsh still watching me and wondered how he knew that Dad had gone away.

When I got outside Jack was sitting down on the step behind the newspaper stand. I unscrewed the top of the Coke and we took turns swigging from the bottle. I laughed when the fizz spurted out of his mouth and went on his T-shirt; he laughed when I tipped too far and the drink went up my nose.

I sat down beside him. We kicked the tyres on our bikes, talked about what we would buy with the rest of the money, what we would buy if we had a pound, what we would buy if we had a hundred. I said I'd buy a Scalextric with so much track that it would go around our house twice. Jack said he'd get another Spitfire. I said he would have enough for ten.

'I mean a real one,' he said.

'You can't afford that.'

'Too late,' he said. 'I've already got one.'

He put the bottle on the ground, stood up and put his arms out wide. I started to laugh as he flew across the squares on the pavement. I stood up and he buzzed around in front of me, humming the drone of the engine and cracking the sound of machine-gun fire.

D-d-d-d-d-d-la. D-d-d-d-d-d-la.
!
D-d-d-d-d-d-la. D-d-d-d-d-d-la.
OK. OK.

I held out my arms and we flew around together in circles outside the shop, then crossed the road into the chip shop, buzzed all the people in the queue and came back out again.

We soared towards the sun.

We dived towards the ground.

Jack got tired.

I got thirsty.

We shut down our propellers and glided back to the shop. We stopped and looked at each other and suddenly felt bad, because for ten minutes, while we were talking and flying, we had forgotten all about the Russians in the sky.

We finished our drinks in silence, then Jack said he wanted some gobstoppers. I gave him the change and told him he could get me some chewing gum at the same time.

I sat in the sun and watched as the newspaper delivery van arrived. A bald man got out, threw a bundle of papers onto the pavement in front of me. Mr Marsh came out of the shop with a knife. He bent down and cut the string around the bundle. I watched as he unfolded a piece of paper and trapped it underneath the wire on the newspaper stand. He whistled as he picked up the papers and went back inside.

Jack came back out with his cheeks stuffed fat like a hamster. He handed me a packet with three gobstoppers in it.

'I wanted gum,' I said.

He juggled his sweets with his tongue.

'Ih was all ey ad.' He laughed.

A purple gobstopper popped out of his mouth and pinged on the pavement. He chased after it as it rolled over the squares on the pavement until he stopped it with his foot.

'You can't eat it,' I said.

He didn't reply. He just stood staring at the newspaper stand.

'What's wrong?' I asked.

He spat his gobstoppers out, lifted up his T-shirt and wiped his dribble from his chin.

'Jack, what does it say?'

He shook his head slowly.

'The Russians are suff . . . The Russians are . . .'

I got up, stood by his side and read the words in my head. But no matter how many times I read them they wouldn't sink in.

'What's it say?' Jack tugged my arm. 'What's it say? Beep.'

'The Russians are suffocating, Jack. That's what it says.'

'What does it mean?'

'It means they can't breathe.'

'Like my asthma?'

'No. It means their oxygen is running out.'

'And that's not the same?'

'No.'

Jack knelt down in front of the board, as if seeing the words up close would help him understand.

'Jack,' I said, 'I think we need to get back.'

He stood up and looked at the sky.

'Why can't they breathe?' he asked.

'I don't know,' I said. 'They might have a hole in their rocket.'

'Can't they glue it back together?'

'I think they're trying.' I looked at the sky with him.

'Can you see them?'

'No,' I said. 'The sun's too bright.'

I bent down, helped him lift his bike, then lifted mine and together we pushed them home.

Chapter Fourteen

The road stretches out in front of us, runs between hedges, falls down hills, winds through valleys and climbs up the other side. We hang our head out the window and the wind rushes by like trains. We look ahead to the horizon, wait for the sky to turn blue and wish that after two hours in Harriet's van we could finally smell the sea. We look across at her. She smiles then jigs up and down in her seat.

'You must know this one,' she says.

?

?

The sound of a piano comes out of the radio.

'You'll get it in a minute.' Harriet turns the music up.

We listen to a man sing a song about killing another man with a gun. We tap our fingers on our bag.

Harriet looks across at us.

'Have you got it?'

We push out our bottom lip.

And we shake our head.

Harriet laughs.

'Bloody hell,' she says. 'Where have you been? It's been number one all summer.'

Well . . .

Don't!

She taps the steering wheel, starts to sway from side to side. Then she starts to sing—

Like a cat.

!

We rest our head against the window. This is the tenth song we have listened to. This is the tenth song she has tried to sing. We wish we knew the words, we wish we knew the tunes, but the only music we have listened to since Dad left has been drowned out by screams and drums.

We look across at Harriet; she smiles like she thinks she is good. The music gets louder, she opens her mouth wider and, just when we think the song has finished, it starts up again.

She's giving us a headache.

——

We put our hands over our ears.

'Oi! It's not that bad.' Harriet punches us on the arm and laughs.

We fall against the door.

It hurts.

I know.

We rub our arm and hope she will do it again.

?

It means she likes us.

Does it? . . . Does that mean Frost liked us too?

No.

We look out the window while Harriet keeps singing the longest song we have ever heard. In the distance a yellow train filled with coal runs along a track through the middle of a valley. The track looks like a zip.

The train looks like a toy.

It's so small that we could pick it up and put it on another line. It reminds us of the last time we went to the beach, when we went by train because Dad couldn't drive. He kept tapping his feet.

He was trying to make the train go faster.

Mum put her hand on his knee, said it was too noisy, that people were watching. Dad looked at us and laughed. He pretended to cut a hole in the floor and started to pedal.

And so did we.

———

Like the Flintstones.

———

The yellow train starts to slow, stops at a platform next to a power station where smoke blows from white towers.

I feel happy.

I feel sad.

Are we happy and sad?

Yes.

Like it's rainy and sunny?

261

Yes, like it's rainy and sunny at the same time.

'Oi!' A finger jabs us in the ribs. We turn around. Harriet has one hand on the steering wheel and the other in the air, finger pointed ready to jab us again. 'What about this one?'

We rub our side and listen to the radio.

Do we know this one?

—

A man sings a song about a season in the sun.

Do we?

No.

—

—

Do you think she's got The Jungle Book?

I doubt it.

I'll ask.

D—

Have you got The Jungle Book?

!

'What?'

Have you got The Jungle Book?

Harriet laughs. We laugh, rest our back against the door and watch her drive. Sometimes she sings.

Sometimes she smiles.

Sometimes she just stares at the road.

The van starts to go uphill, she presses the clutch down, puts her hand on the gearstick. The sound of metal crashing grates through the van. She pulls her hand away like she's just been stung.

'You're putting me off,' she says.

We're only watching.

I was only watching.

We look out the side window. Harriet puts her hand on our knee.

We jump.

'It's OK.' She smiles. 'I was only joking.'

She takes her hand away and even though it has gone we feel a tingle in the spot she touched.

We smile, look back at her. She starts to rock backwards and forwards.

!

!

'Oh no!'

!

Sorry.

'No, it's not you.' She presses the accelerator flat to the floor and points at the dashboard. 'It's the radiator.'

We lean over. A needle creeps from cold to hot on the temperature gauge.

!

Is it bad?

'Yes, it's bad.' She glances in the side mirror and for the first time we see she is worried. We look behind, see clouds of smoke billowing out the side of the van, leaving a trail back down the hill.

It's going to explode!

—

Harriet rocks backwards and forwards, tries to make us go faster.

'Come on,' she says. 'Fucking come on.'

She shouldn't—

Don't . . .

'Sorry.'

The engine rattles, the exhaust starts to growl. Harriet bangs her hand on the steering wheel, stares straight ahead at the road as it keeps climbing until it disappears like a cliff edge into the sky.

'Not here. Not here.'

The van goes slower, starts to vibrate through our body. We crawl past hedges and trees and the smoke is now so thick it's like we're stuck in a cloud.

We think that we might have to get out.

But—

We think we might have to get out and push.

'Yes!' Harriet leans back, blows out her cheeks as the van crests the top of the hill. 'Made it.'

We all smile and breathe out as the van starts to quicken and we roll down the other side.

Harriet flicks the indicator on when we reach the bottom.

What are we doing?

What are we doing?

———

Harriet points at the temperature gauge.

'We've got to stop for water to help cool it down,' she says.

But we're still going to the beach?

!

Harriet shakes her head and laughs. 'You're funny,' she says.

The van starts to turn, lurches down into a dip. We all bounce up and down in the seat as the tyres search for grip over tractor tracks. We fall forward and our bag slides off the seat as Harriet jams on the brakes. The smoke circles around us. Harriet turns off the engine.

———

———

'Don't look so worried,' she says. 'It does it all the time.' She looks over her shoulder into the back of the van. 'I just need to check we've got water.'

She climbs between the seats. We look out the window, watch the smoke clear away and look over a gate into a field. The van starts to rock. We hear the sound of a muffled voice coming from a cupboard and look over our shoulder. Harriet leans out, her face is red and her fringe has flopped over her eyes.

'My dad's filled it to the top. Can you help me?'

We climb into the back. Harriet points at a yellow water container. We try to reach it but there is not enough space for us all between the cupboard and the cooker. She smiles.

'I think I'd better get out of the way,' she says. She squeezes past. We feel her breath on our face and the warmth of her body as it presses against ours. We feel ourself turn red. Harriet opens the side door and steps out onto the grass.

We stand alone in the van, see a blue sleeping bag rolled up on a seat, see a pair of red pyjamas folded by the side—

And a little bag.

We bend down and pick up a book with NHS written across the top and a picture of a nurse underneath. A car rushes by and rocks the van.

——

——

We look out the door, see patches of Harriet's yellow dress between the green of the hedge.

Is she looking?

I think she's peeing.

?

We open the book.

This book is the property of Harriet Jones.

I don't think we should be doing this.

We have to.

It'll give us something to talk about.

Oh.

We flip over the page, see scratches of blue ink, Harriet's tiny spidery writing scrawled across a diagram of the human heart.

'Tom!' Harriet's voice sounds loud, like she's used a microphone in the wind.

We turn around and see her standing with her elbows resting on a gate.

'It's boring stuff,' she says.

We flip the book shut.

Sorry.

Sorry.

'It's OK.'

The book slips off the seat onto the floor. We bend down and pick it up. Our blood thuds in our head.

Because we've been caught?

Because we've seen a little piece of her.

We stand in the van not knowing where to look or go.

Harriet laughs. 'I said it's OK . . . . It's just work, it's not like you've sniffed my knickers.'

!

!

We look down at the container.

'Leave it in the shade,' she says. We lift it out onto

the grass then pick up our bag. Harriet grins, turns away and we wish there was a breeze to cool our face down. We climb over the gate and follow her through the footprints of cows. In the middle of the field she stops, turns in a circle and looks up at the sky.

'It takes ages.'

?

?

'The radiator – my dad says I have to leave it an hour to cool down.'

She should use nitrogen.

——

She should use nitrogen.

You should use nitrogen.

That's what I said.

'Ha! What are you, a scientist?'

——

Not really.

She bends down, taps her hand on the ground, then sits on the grass. We slip our bag off our shoulder and sit down opposite her. She laughs.

'You look like you're in school assembly.'

?

Oh.

We uncross our legs. Harriet puts her hands behind her head. Her dress creeps up over her knees as she closes her eyes and lies back on the grass.

The wind rustles the hedges, blows around our head.

In the distance we hear the sound of lorry crawling up
the hill.

———

———

———

———

This is a bit boring.

———

———

We watch Harriet breathe.

We look around the field.

!

———

Can we play something?

No.

——— ———

———

———

We spy with our little eye—

Not We spy again.

Harriet opens her eyes and looks at us. 'Why don't
you lie down?' she says. 'You're twitching like a rabbit.'

Sorry.

Sorry.

'What are you doing?'

Playing 'We spy'.

'I spy'!

'*I spy.*'

She looks at us like she doesn't understand.

You can play too.

She doesn't want to.

She does.

'OK.'

Told you.

!

I'll go first.

!

I spy . . . I spy with our little eye——

Camper van.

That's not fair.

'Hurry up,' says Harriet.

I spy with our little eye something beginning with s——

Sky.

Harriet looks back to the gate, follows the hedge around the field.

'S,' she says. 'S . . .'

It's sky.

It's not.

It is.

Harriet bites her bottom lip.

'S . . . S . . . Stethoscope!'

Yes.

What? Where?

——

I'm not playing any more.

Harriet laughs and lies back down again.

—

—

—

!

?

Hangman?

No.

—

—

We could go and explore.

We could just sit here.

—

—

We stand up, look across the field to where it gently slopes away until the edge is out of sight. We walk down the slope, hear the sound of running water. A stream flows down the hill over stones and boulders. We sit down and take off our socks and trainers.

Are we going to make a dam?

No, we're going to wash.

?

Because we stink.

Oh.

We take off our T-shirt and jumper and leave them on the bank,

So we're going to wash.

That's what I said.

. . . And then we're going to make a dam.

!

Harriet sleeps in the sun. We open our bag, take out our book and our planes and put them on the grass.

I don't want to wear our Arsenal shirt.

Shush!

I don't want to wear our Arsenal shirt.

It's all we've got.

Can't we just wear our jumper?

No.

Because it's too hot?

Because it itches our skin.

We pick up our Arsenal shirt, put our arms through and pull the neck down over our wet hair.

'Where have you been?' Harriet opens her eyes and squints in the sun.

Down to the stream.

We reach back into our bag and put on a jumper.

Harriet sits up and picks our book up off the grass. 'What's this?' she asks.

She looks at our drawing on the front. We wait for her to laugh but she just sits without speaking, running her hand over the cover. A weird feeling grows inside us, a tingle that sends a shiver up our spine.

Because she is looking at something about us?

Yes.

'"Our Book", by Tom and Jack Gagarin.' She looks up, shakes her head slowly. 'I should have known,' she says. 'The mysterious writer.'

We smile then look at the ground.

—

'Which one's you?'

That one.

And that one.

'I like the yellow hair.'

!

I didn't draw it.

'Who did?'

—

Jack.

'Is that him?'

Yes.

'Are you twins?'

Ha! See.

No, but he was my brother.

'Was?'

—

He died.

!

Harriet lifts her head. 'Oh . . . I'm sorry. I didn't mean to—'

It's OK.

Is it?

'No, I shouldn't have—' She goes quiet and looks at us as if she likes us more.

———

———

She runs her hand over the cover one more time. 'Here.' She holds it out. 'I was being nosy . . . I can't help it. I shouldn't have looked.'

We reach out, hold one end of the book while she holds the other. We think that we'd like her to read it, that we'd like her to know about Mum and Dad.

We'd like her to look at the pictures.

We'd like her to tell us if our book is any good.

———

———

You can read it if you like.

'Are you sure?'

Are we?

Yes.

———

Harriet puts our book on her lap and opens the cover.

'Ha! I like this,' she says.

What's that?

What's that?

'This . . .'

Ha!

!

She smiles, flicks over to the first chapter and starts to read.

"'It was hot but I was cold the day after Jack died.'"

Have we got to start again?

!

We've read this bit sixteen times!

Harriet laughs.

'You wrote it,' she says.

She rolls over onto her stomach. We roll over onto ours. Harriet shakes her head, rubs it against our shoulder.

'You're weird,' she says.

?

?

We flip forward to our marker. Harriet puts her fingers on the page to stop it turning in the wind.

'Shall I start?'

Yes.

Yes.

We lean in closer and start to read.

Summer 1971

The desert was grey in Kazakhstan. The Russians' capsule lay in the sand. Three helicopters hovered in the blue sky and a voice crackled over a radio.

Sporry wurry sputnik. Beep beep glitsch.

That was the Russians.

!

Harriet looks at us then back at the page.

I think she can read it on her own.

OK.

Me and Jack crawled closer to the TV. The capsule was tilted on its side. Black burn marks licked from the bottom to the door and stopped at the window. A parachute was stretched out like spilt oil on the sand. I remembered what I'd read in my encyclopaedia about Commander Komarov, how Soyuz 1's parachute didn't open and the spaceship kept spinning until it fell out of the sky.

I put my arm around Jack. The Russians had landed safely this time.

A commentator started talking.

'This is the moment the world has been waiting for,' he said. 'After holding our breaths for two days, the Russians are finally coming home.'

I looked at Jack and he smiled. We'd been holding our breaths for longer than everyone else, we'd been holding ours all summer.

An army truck with big wheels drove across the sand and stopped. Two men wearing white boiler suits jumped out and ran over to the capsule. One looked in through the window, the other reached out and tried the handle on the door. He wriggled it up and down but the door wouldn't open. The first man tried, then they tried together, but the door still didn't open. They looked up at the helicopters, waved their arms and tried the door again. The helicopters came down from the sky and blasted the sand into clouds that I couldn't see through. The two men knelt down as the helicopters came in to land. I felt sweat trickle down the side of my face and my heart started to thud because after waiting twenty-eight days for them to come home it seemed like the Russians were trapped inside. I wondered if it was because they were weak, that a lunar month of eating pills had made them thin.

'It could be gravity,' said the commentator. 'It could simply be that gravity is weighing them down.'

There were now four men in white suits standing by the capsule. One jammed an iron bar against the door, the other three stood and watched. Then the commentator spoke again, but this time it was a whisper.

'We've received a message from the Russians,' he said. 'It's an unconfirmed report . . . a rumour.' Then he stopped like he was taking a big breath in the middle of his sentence.

Jack nudged me. 'What's a rumour?' he asked.

'It means that he's heard something but he can't be certain.'

'This information has come to us from Moscow,' said the commentator. 'It's feared that—'

Sporry wurry sputnik. Beep. Beep. Glitsch!

I leant forward, put my head against the speaker. My ear crackled with the sound of static.

'It's thought the cosmonauts . . . It's thought they may have suffocated.'

Jack pulled my arm.

'What did he say?'

I tried to answer but all my thoughts were fighting inside my head, spinning like the rotor blades. Jack screwed up his face and bit the skin on his fingers.

'It's only a rumour,' I said. 'It might not be true.'

He bit harder. I didn't want him to cry but I could see the tears growing in the corners of his eyes.

Another man grabbed hold of the bar.

'They'll be OK,' I said. 'The door's just jammed, it might have melted on re-entry, and when they open it up they'll find Dad, Viktor and Georgi laughing inside.'

He tried to smile but from the sad look on his face I could tell he didn't believe what I'd said, and when I saw the men in white boiler suits shaking their heads, neither did I.

The TV picture started to flicker. I heard music play quietly, drums and trumpets, but the drummers were too tired to beat and the trumpeters were too scared to blow. Another truck drove across the sand and stopped. I couldn't see the capsule any more. The music got quieter and slowly the picture faded away.

I pressed a button on the TV, then another and another, but all I could find were fuzzy pictures and the sound of white noise. I didn't know what to do. I thought maybe I'd misheard the commentator, or maybe he was deaf and had misheard the rumour. A hundred thoughts rushed through my head at the same time. I wondered how it could have happened, that maybe Dad had got tired and pressed the wrong button, or Georgi should have changed direction, flown over Kazakhstan and landed in the Pacific Ocean. My body started to shake. I wanted to tell someone, someone who could help. I turned around. Auntie Jean was asleep on the settee with her mouth open. I looked at Jack and thought of asking him but if I couldn't understand then neither could he.

I crawled across the floor and climbed up onto a chair. Jack squeezed in beside me. I couldn't say anything, all I could think of was the Russians and Dad and the word 'suffocate'. I put my arm around Jack and we waited for Mum to come home.

I felt a tickle on my face, like an ant crawling from my neck up to my eye.

I scratched my cheek and rolled over.

I felt the tickle again and heard the faint sound of a soft voice calling my name.

I opened my eyes. The sitting room was dark, full of silhouettes and shadows.

'Tom.'

Mum was kneeling on the floor with her chin resting on the arm of my chair. I blinked. She smiled and gently rubbed her hand over mine.

'It's late,' she whispered.

I looked around the sitting room, started to get up.

'Where's—'

'He's OK,' she said. 'I took him up to bed.' She rubbed her hand up my arm like she was trying to flatten the chicken bumps on my skin. 'You're cold,' she said.

I stared ahead at the TV, the blank black screen in the corner, and remembered all the pictures of the Russians I'd seen during the afternoon. A horrible feeling grew deep inside me, an ache, a throbbing ache around my heart, like a balloon filled with water was going to explode in my chest. The word 'suffocate' kept whispering through my head over and over again.

I'd woken from a nightmare and found out it was true.

Tears started to fall down my cheeks. Mum held me tighter.

'Tom, what's wrong?'

The feeling came again, like a wave through my body. I swallowed.

'Dad's dead,' I said.

Mum put her hand on my head and started to rock me from side to side.

'No,' she said. 'No. Dad's not dead, he's just gone away.'

'But he came back. The Russians came back.'

'Hush,' she said. She held me close to her chest until my crying words were smothered against her. 'It'll be OK,' she said. 'Everything will be OK.'

I wanted to talk, I wanted to tell her everything that had happened to Dad and the Russians since she'd been gone. But the more I thought about it, the worse the pain got.

I felt the warmth of Mum's breath, I heard the thump of her heart. I closed my eyes and wished Dad was back and that the pain would go away.

There were pictures of tanks and marching bands carrying red flags on the TV when I woke up the next morning. Writing kept flashing up on the screen:

LIVE FROM MOSCOW'S RED SQUARE.

Two photographs the size of our house hung from the roofs of red buildings – two men in uniform with red stripes on their hats and gold stars on their arms. I stared at the screen and saw the faces of Georgi and Viktor staring back at me.

Jack shuffled beside me. We looked at the pictures and I read the numbers written underneath.

'It's the dates they were born,' I said, 'and the dates that they died.'

He nodded like he understood.

The camera moved across the square, over the top of tanks and horses, over the heads of the soldiers, and stopped when it reached a red building with gold turrets on top. A photograph hung from the roof down to the ground. I didn't want to look. I didn't want to see a picture of Dad. The music got louder, cymbals and trumpets and drums.

I heard someone sniff and turned around. Mum was standing in the doorway, her face was white and her eyes were red like a rabbit's. She wiped her nose on a tissue.

'Boys, there's something I've got to tell you.'

She came in and sat on the floor behind us. The drums drummed, the cymbals clashed. The giant photograph flapped gently in the wind. I put my hands up to my face and peeped through my fingers at a man in a uniform with shiny buttons on his shoulders and little flags and medals pinned to his chest. A big grin stretched across his face. I took my hands down. Jack nudged my arm.

'It's not Dad,' he said.

I stared at the face, at the man's brown eyes, his black hair.

'I know,' I said. 'I know.'

'Who is it then?'

I read the name and the dates written underneath.

VLADISLAV NIKOLAYEVICH VOLKOV
NOVEMBER 23, 1935–JUNE 30, 1971

I shook my head. I didn't understand, I suddenly felt happy and sad at the same time. Mum sat on the floor beside me.

'It's not Dad,' I said.

'I know,' she whispered and shook her head slowly.

The music stopped playing.

The tanks stopped moving.

And the soldiers stood still.

A man shouted something backwards and the soldiers pointed their rifles and shot three times into the sky.

'So where is he?' I whispered. 'Where's Dad?'

Mum's lips started to move but no words came out.

The soldiers started marching, the music started playing, the pictures of Georgi, Viktor and Vladislav were moved together until they took up the whole screen.

Mum got up and sat on the settee. Me and Jack got up and sat beside her as the pictures and music started to fade away. Mum took a deep breath.

'I don't know where to start,' she said.

Me and Jack waited for her to speak but all she did was wrap her arms around us and stare at the TV.

The scientist came back on. He pointed at a diagram of the moon and traced the line that went back to Earth. He told us about the mission and showed us a model of Soyuz 11 and a Space Station. He opened up the hatches, joined them together to make a tunnel and then told us how the cosmonauts had crawled through to conduct their experiments on the other side.

'This is where the leak may have occurred.' He pointed at a circle of metal on the hatch of Soyuz 11. 'It may have melted in the atmosphere, or the Russians may not have sealed it properly when they undocked from the Space Station.'

He pointed at the model again. He said that the Russians may have run out of money when they built the rocket, that they may have used spare parts from tanks and cars. He drew a graph on a board and wrote a complicated equation underneath that I didn't understand. I looked back at the model. There were three cosmonauts sitting on one side of the tunnel and one sitting on his own at the other end. My heart started thumping and my head started spinning like rockets, Space Stations and satellites were flying around me.

I stood up.

'He's OK,' I said. 'Dad's OK.'

Jack looked at me like I'd gone mad. Mum shook her head.

'No, Tom,' she said.

'He is,' I said. 'He is.'

I walked over to the TV, pointed at the rocket, the Space Station and the tunnel where the hatches joined together. I pointed at the three cosmonauts in the capsule, then at the other one in the Space Station.

'It's obvious,' I said. 'Dad isn't dead. He's just been left behind.'

Mum put her hand up to her mouth.

'No, Tom,' she said. 'That's not . . . I don't think—'

'It is,' I said. 'It is.' I looked at Jack; his eyebrows were pushed together like he still hadn't worked it out. I pointed at the TV again.

'See, Jack. Three cosmonauts . . . And Dad doing experiments on the other side.'

Jack started to smile.

We both looked at Mum.

'I'm right,' I said. 'I worked it out.'

Jack got up and stood by my side.

'He's always right.'

Mum's hands started to shake and her eyes glistened like glass.

'Isn't he, Mum?'

Mum stared at me, like she was still thinking, then slowly she started to nod.

'Yes,' she said. 'I think Tom might be right.'

That night I dragged my blanket across our bedroom and me and Jack sat together on his bed. We opened our book and read Dad's letters from the moon over and over again. We thought how lonely he must be now Viktor and Georgi were gone and wondered how long he would be able to survive in space on his own. He'd said in one of his letters that he could hold his breath for two minutes.

I pulled back the curtain, looked up at the sky and tried to find a light that might be the Space Station flickering between the stars. I hoped Dad could try and take deep slow breaths, that maybe he'd find a little pocket of oxygen in the corner by the switches, that he could stay alive for days like sailors when their boats turn upside down in the sea.

A cloud crossed the moon. I heard the rustle of pages, turned around and saw Jack flicking through our book like he wanted to get to the end before he went to sleep.

'Don't tear it,' I said.

He kept turning the pages, his hand moving so fast it started to blur.

'What are you looking for?'

'This,' he said. He pulled a piece of paper out of the back of our book and jumped out of his bed.

HOW TO BUILD A ROCKET BY STEVE GAGARIN

I looked at the page, at the diagram of wires going into boxes then coming out the other side and going into a washing machine and a fridge. All the parts Dad had used for his rocket were written in a long list underneath. A big smile crept across Jack's face. I looked out the window and up at our hill. The silhouette of Dad's launch site stuck up like castle walls in the dark.

'Can we do it?' Jack whispered. 'Can we build the rocket?'

I looked back at the diagram.

'I don't know,' I said. 'It's complicated.'

I looked back at the piece of paper, at the lines looping across the page, over and under each other, like a puzzle where you guide the mouse to the cheese. Dad always said it wasn't easy, he said if it was easy everyone would be building rockets. I looked back up at the hill, then at the sky.

'We could try, Jack.' I said. 'I think we should try.'

I jumped as our bedroom door clicked open. Mum put her head around the side.

'I thought you'd be sleeping,' she said. She walked in and stood between us at the window.

'We're going to build a rocket,' said Jack. He smiled and looked as excited as I felt inside.

Mum looked up at the hill and slowly shook her head.

'You can't,' she said. 'Someone's telephoned the council, they're taking it all away in the morning.'

'But they can't,' I said. 'It's Dad's rocket . . . And I've got the instructions.'

She took them out of my hand. Her eyes moved side to side as she followed all the wires then she stopped and whispered the words written underneath. 'Trust no one . . . Tell no one . . . They might be spies.' Dad had written it ten times.

Mum folded the instructions and gave them back to me.

'I'm sorry,' she said. She kissed us both goodnight then walked out and closed the door.

I sat on Jack's bed and looked at my clock on my wall. It was still stuck on T minus zero.

'Are we still going to build it?' Jack whispered.

'I'm thinking,' I said.

'But we've not got long left.'

'I know.'

'They're going to take it away.'

'I know . . . I know . . .'

I stopped talking as Mum's footsteps crossed the landing into the bathroom.

'We can't rush it,' I said. 'Mum always says—'

'Good things come to those who wait.'

'Yes.' I lay down on my bed, tried to figure out everything we had to do, knowing that all the while I was thinking, time was disappearing. I didn't know what to do. The person I wanted to ask was the person I was trying to help. It was too late to send Dad a letter, it'd never reach him in time.

The toilet flushed. Mum went back into her bedroom and clicked off the light.

I couldn't let the council take the rocket, but we couldn't take off without being prepared. I got up, put on my dressing gown and slippers. Jack jumped out of his bed and did the same.

'What are we going to do?'

'We can't let them take it,' I whispered. 'We've got to get it down.'

We crept towards the door.

'But where are we going to put it?'

'Somewhere safe,' I said.

'But where?'

'The back garden.'

I pulled the door open, looked left towards the bathroom and looked right towards Mum's bedroom. The coast was clear. We crept onto the landing and down the stairs. Dad had taken the whole of the summer to take the rocket up the hill. Me and Jack only had one night to bring it all down.

Chapter Fifteen

Tom.

Tom!

What?

Can we go now?

____

Can we go now? Beep.

. . . We can't.

Why not?

Harriet says it's too late.

?

She doesn't like driving in the dark.

But what about Dad?

____

What about Dad? Beep.

We'll find him tomorrow.

I can't wait that long.

You'll have to.

Why?

____

Why? Beep.

Because she's just made us tea.

—

Harriet passes us a bowl and sits down beside us. We pick up a fork, twist it in our spaghetti, our elbow knocks against hers. She smiles, we smile. Our elbows knock again.

It's like we're back at Mrs Drummond's.

It's like we're fighting for space in a submarine.

'So, what happens next?' Harriet nods at the bench where our book lies open on the last page we read. 'What happens now that the Russians have come home?'

Can I tell her?

I thought you wanted to leave.

We built a rocket.

!

In our garden.

—

Out of a fridge and a washing machine. Then—

I think that's enough.

But—

We shove a spoonful of spaghetti into our mouth. Harriet smiles.

'You're a good writer,' she says. 'I'd be rubbish. I haven't got any imagination.'

?

?

'How did you make it all up?'

It's true.

Shush!

But it is.

'Ha!' Harriet puts her hand up to her mouth, coughs and laughs at the same time.

?

!

Her face goes red and her eyes start to water. 'I'm sorry,' she says. 'I'm not laughing at you.' She takes a drink.

We look down, turn our fork in the bowl.

'I didn't mean it.' She puts her hand on our arm.

It's OK.

!

She smiles, we smile, and we think how pretty she looks with tears in her eyes. We sit in silence and look out the back window at the car lights crawling up the hill, they look like people carrying lanterns. The camper-van light flickers. We look up at the ceiling like we're looking for ghosts.

'It's OK,' she says. 'We've just got to save the battery or we'll still be stuck here tomorrow.'

But we can't . . .

!

She gets up, opens the cupboard and lights a candle. We watch as she walks towards us with her tongue poking out, trying not to blow out the flame. She switches the light off and sits back down beside us.

We sit in the dark surrounded by shadows.

'Oh,' she says.

We jump.

'I nearly forgot.' She leans forward, reaches under the bench and slides out a cardboard box.

Ludo?

———

Snakes and ladders?

'Here.' She lifts up four bottles of beer.

Oh.

'We can share these.'

She opens a drawer and finds a bottle opener.

'You do it,' she says. 'I've just got to go outside.'

———

Shall I come?

'No,' she says. 'I just need the loo.'

She opens the door and steps out. We pick up a bottle.

I think we should go now.

Why?

I want to find Dad.

I told you. Tomorrow.

I won't help you open the bottle then.

I don't need your help.

!

The bottle opener slips off the top and onto the floor.

I don't like it when we meet people.

———

You don't listen to me.

———

You don't listen to me. Beep.

Shush!

Harriet steps back inside with her arms folded across her chest.

'It's a bit cold,' she says. She sits down close to us like she wants to get warm.

'Don't tell me you don't drink?' She nods at the bottles.

We don't.

———

We show her our bandaged hand.

'Oh, sorry, I forgot.'

She prises the tops off two bottles and curls her feet up on the bench. We take a drink, then Harriet takes a drink, and leans against us, rests her head on our shoulder.

!

———

She wriggles, makes an umm sound like she's trying to get comfortable on a pillow.

'This is nice,' she says.

?

———

We want to lie back.

We want to go!

We want to close our eyes, we want to touch her hair, we want to lift our arm and put it around her.

But we're not going to.

We might.

!

Harriet puts her hand on our chest and sighs.

'I don't want to go back,' she says.

Nor do we.

———

'I don't even want to be a bloody nurse.'

She takes a swig from her bottle. We take one from ours and listen to Harriet.

'It was my dad's idea. He said I needed to find a career, but he just wanted me out of the house . . . but only because she's there.' She takes another swig. 'Bitch . . . I hate her.'

!

Who?

'His new girlfriend.'

———

———

We take another swig of our beer. Harriet nestles in closer, makes a quick huffing sound like she's going to laugh. 'You might be quiet, but you're a bloody good listener.' She lifts her head and stares into our eyes.

Can we turn the torch on?

!

'What?'

I think we should turn the torch on.

Harriet laughs. 'You are funny,' she says.

Are we?

Am I?

'Yes. Sometimes.'

She brushes her fingers across our cheek.

'Wouldn't it nice if we could just stay here?'

No.

——

We lie back. Harriet puts her head on our chest. Our heart beats slowly through our body.

Can we go—

I think you should go to sleep.

Is it half past ten?

I think so.

But you don't know?

I think it might be later.

We yawn.

Will you keep guard?

Yes.

Like a soldier?

Ha!

?

I knew you were listening.

I always am.

——

Goodnight.

Goodnight.

——

——

'This isn't very comfortable.' Harriet puts the drinks on the drainer then puts her hands under the table. We get up. The table goes down level with the bench and we help her slide a mattress on top.

'That's better,' she says.

We climb on the bed. Harriet pours water in a kettle and lights the gas.

We lie back, put our hands behind our head and think of the bed we have left behind, the one on wheels that kept creeping to the door. We think of our room, wonder if someone new is already sleeping in it. We wonder if they have read our writing on the wall, if they are listening to James Lewis crying on the other side like we used to do. We think of Frost in the corner, picking his nails, looking at his picture— Oh shit, Frost! A scream pierces through our head. Our hands start to shake and a line of sweat creeps down the side of our face. We sit up.

Harriet puts one hand on the mattress.

'Are you OK?'

—

'You look worried.' She puts her hand on our shoulder.

We catch our breath.

Yes.

'It's all right,' she says. 'We'll just lie together.'

She opens a cupboard, pulls out a sleeping bag and puts it on the bed.

We reach for it, slide down inside and pull it up to our chin. Harriet turns off the kettle, pours water in the sink. We watch her silhouette move from one side of the van to the other, unzipping a little bag, unscrewing a cap on a little bottle. She opens the cupboard door and starts to get undressed behind it.

Her dress falls to the floor.

We smell her perfume and soap in hot water.

The water drains away and she closes the door. For a moment she stands still like she's lost. We see the shape of her head, her hair hanging down her neck, and the gap between her arms, and the curve of her body where the light shines through.

She bends down, creeps to the bench by the side of our feet and puts on her pyjamas. The van shakes as she crawls up the mattress and lies by our side. We stare at the ceiling. Harriet rolls over and we feel her breath on our face.

——

'Tom,' she whispers.

We stay still.

'Tom.'

Yes.

She shuffles closer until her body is pressed against ours. 'I'm cold,' she says. 'Can we cuddle?'

We ease our arm out of our sleeping bag and wrap

it around her. She puts her head on our chest. We run our hand through her hair and she lets out a little giggle.

What's wrong?

'Nothing.' She giggles again.

What is it?

'Why have you still got your clothes on?'

We try to think of an answer but it's hard when the one who does most of the talking is now sleeping.

—

A quick getaway.

'From me?'

From anyone.

She moves her foot and knocks it against ours.

'And your trainers?'

It takes too long for us to tie the laces.

'Us?'

Me.

—

—

—

'Can I ask you something?' Her voice is a whisper.

?

'Your book, is it really true?'

Yes.

'All of it?'

We nod.

'Will I be in it?'

It's finished, we— I just read it.

'Sixteen times.' She laughs.

Yes, sixteen times.

'Why?'

Because sometimes I forget.

'How?'

——

'What happens?'

——

——

We sigh. Harriet takes a deep breath like she's going to say something. We turn our head towards the window.

——

——

Harriet leans over, puts her finger on our chin and smiles.

'What . . . What would you say about me?'

——

'Would you say that I talk too much?'

No.

'But I do?'

Yes, but not as much as someone I know.

——

'I talk when I'm nervous,' she says. 'I can't help it.'

I like it.

'Because I'm funny?'

Because it gives me time to think of what to say.

She laughs.

———

'I wish I could go to the beach with you.'

———

'I could phone college, tell them we can't get started.'

———

We close our eyes. We wish we could do this all the time. We wish we could travel with Harriet. She could stop going to college, we could stop running away. We think about tomorrow, what we will do when we get to the beach, how one of us wants to look for Dad and play in the sand while the other wants to sit on the dunes and watch the waves. We screw our eyes up tight, see shades of colour, see shapes of shadows that turn into aeroplanes and rockets and Mum and Dad when we were all at home. I think how everything has changed since that summer. I think of all the places I have been since the night I went to bed as me and woke up as us.

———

Harriet nestles her head further into our shoulder.
'We'll decide in the morning.'
We yawn, our eyes are heavy and tired. We know we shouldn't go to sleep, we know one of us has to stand guard, but we think it's OK.

———

Isn't it?

We put our hand on Harriet's head. Her fingers crawl down our neck onto our body. We turn over on our side; the candle flame flickers across her face, catches one eye, casts a small shadow of her nose. She smiles again. We feel ourself shaking, try to stop it. She smooths our hair, presses her body against ours and her fingers go up over our cheek towards our temple.

We put our hand on top of hers.

'What's wrong?'

We can't let her touch our temple, the burn marks might have gone like our memory, but the scars are still there.

'It's OK,' she says.

—

—

—

We close our eyes.

—

—

—

—

Intruder alert! Intruder alert!

—

Intruder alert! Intruder alert!

What?

Intruder alert.

It's not.

It is.

It's just Harriet.

'What is it? What is it?'

She hasn't got any clothes on.

—

Oh shit!

What?

Neither have we.

Harriet sits up. 'Tom, who are you talking to?'

It's nothing.

She's naked. We're naked.

It's OK, it's OK.

'What the—'

Harriet scrambles to the end of the bed and turns on the light.

See! Intruder alert! Intruder alert!

Jack! Don't do this. Not again.

Harriet puts her hand over her mouth. 'Oh my God.'

We've got to find our dad. We've got to find our dad.

In the morning, Jack. We'll find him in the morning.

Now, we've got to go now.

We put on our trousers, pull our T-shirt and jumper over our head.

Harriet picks up her sleeping bag and hides behind it.

We've got to go, we've got to find our dad.

I'm sorry.

We're sorry.

Harriet screws up her face like she's going to cry.

We look around the van.

Our book, our book. We need our book.

——

And our rockets and our planes.

We put our hands on our head.

Harriet opens her mouth.

Don't scream.

Don't scream.

We pick up our book and our bag.

It's just him.

'Who?'

My brother.

Harriet stares at us, starts to shake as tears run down her cheeks.

We slide the door open and look back at her. She sits down on the bed.

I'm sorry.

We're sorry.

We step out into the dark. The grass is cold on our feet and the night air makes us dizzy. We hear the sound of footsteps, the door slamming, then the click of a lock.

Our head aches, our neck starts to throb. We want to shout. We want to scream but everything is trapped inside. We don't want to leave her. We don't want to leave her like we have left everyone else. But we have to, because no one understands, because the more we talk the worse it gets.

—

—

We put our book in our bag and walk out onto the road. The wind rustles through the hedge. We turn round and look through the windscreen of the van, where an orange light glows.

—

—

We think of Harriet inside curled up on her own in the corner. We watch for a moment and then turn away. The road stretches out in front of us, the sky is full of blurry lights. We hear the sound of someone crying.

—

We sniff, wipe our tears from our eyes.

—

—

—

We put our book in our bag, put our bag over our shoulder. Our head begins to thud. Our throat already aches. We walk along the road.

—

I'm sorry.

—

—

I'm—

It's OK.

. . . But it's not really?

—

?

No, it's not really.

Chapter Sixteen

We are tired.

We are tired of running.

We have run through valleys, we have crawled over hills and we have waited for a bus that never came.

We were hungry.

We were thirsty. But we had to keep going as we had come too far to stop.

But we did look back.

—

Just for a minute.

—

We looked back and thought of Harriet.

—

Because if we had stayed in her van we could have been at the beach in an hour.

—

Green fields stretched out in front of us. They turned to brown, then yellow and disappeared into the sea. Cars roared past with rubber dinghies on top.

A girl shouted out the window and showed us her toy crocodile.

We wish we had a crocodile.

We wish they'd given us a lift.

We reached the last hill, smelt the salt in the wind. Our lungs grew big, our heart grew bigger. We swung our bag on our back and rolled like a marble down to the sea.

Now we are standing at the bottom of a sand dune and looking up to the top. It seems too high to climb over and too wide to go around. Mum said that things would seem to get smaller as we got older and taller, but the dune seems bigger than we remember. We look around and wonder if this is the right place because there is no one to follow. We have never got here so early that our footprints were the first ones in the sand.

—

—

But it is?

What?

The right place?

I think so.

We put our bag on our back and start to climb but with every step we take our feet slide back through the sand to where they began.

Like Tom and Jerry.

Like a dog burying a bone.

We sink to our knees and start to crawl. The sand slips between our fingers but sticks to our cut.

Our legs ache.

Sweat stings our eyes.

And I can't breathe.

Neither can I.

We try to fill our lungs but it's like someone has chopped off our head and poured tar inside. We spread our arms wide, we spread our legs wider.

We wish we could stop.

We wish we were geckos.

?

Lizards.

Oh.

We throw our bag in front of us, take off our shirt and wrap it around our head like a pirate.

To stop the flies from eating us?

To stop the heat of the sun.

Are we going to die?

?

Are we going to die?

No.

But I saw it in a film with you and Dad.

?

Men wearing sheets?

?

Lots of camels . . . It was boring.

It was *Lawrence of Arabia.*

And Lawrence died.

But this is a sand dune, not the desert. And he didn't
die there.

How did he die?

I thought you were watching.

I've forgotten.

Keep crawling.

I am.

The sun burns on our back. We look up at the top;
we have been crawling for five minutes but it feels like
we haven't even started. Our sweat drips off our chin
onto the sand. We grab at pieces of grass; they hold us
for a while but then come away in our hands. Our head
seems to be getting hotter the closer we get to the sun.
We take a deep breath and crawl on.

—

—

So how did he die?

?

Lawrence, how did he die?

He crashed his motorbike when two boys ran into
the road.

Ooops!

—

But it wasn't us?

No.

Sand fills our shoes and weighs us down. We take
them off, stand up and throw them along with our bag,

up ahead to where the sky gets wider and the sun flattens out. We put our head down and crawl on.

At the top we kneel down and let the wind cool our face.

Is he here?

—

Is he here?

—

Our head sinks in the sand. Our heart beats in our chest. We breathe deep, screw up our eyes tight and the world turns orange. We try to picture Dad's face, we try to imagine his voice, we try to remember his big hands wrapped around ours as he pulled us through the water.

We look down across the beach out towards the sea, past blankets and windbreaks to where children jump and scream in the waves. Red buoys float up and down in the breakers and trail out in a line towards the horizon. There are no tankers in the heat haze, there are no vapour trails in the sky. We look along the beach towards the rock pools in the distance. They are blue and empty. No one walks through them.

This is the place.

—

Isn't it?

Yes, this is the place. This is the place where we were sharks.

So what do we do now?

What we always do.

?

Wait.

We lie back on our bag and watch the sun burn a hole in the sky.

—

—

Raindrops fall on our skin. We sit up. A cloud bubbles in the sky, then another, and another, until they join together and float across the sea like an army coming towards us.

I think we should run.

A flash of lightning turns a fishing boat black on the grey water.

I don't like—

We clamp our hands over our ears—

1 2 3 4 5 6 7.

We feel the rumble of thunder.

We pick up our book.

Another flash of lightning zigzags across the sky.

123456789 . . . it's going away.

It's because you're counting quicker.

Oh.

We run along the dune with our bag banging on our back and our book clutched tight to our chest. A path dips up and down and weaves in front of us.

Like a snake?

—

Like a roller coaster?

Like the Great Wall of China.

?

Just keep running.

The rain comes down hard, slaps our hair to our head, sticks our shirt to our skin.

. . . What's the Wall of China?

—

Is it the same as the Iron Curtain?

—

Is it the same as—

No.

Our legs start to ache. Our heart thumps hard. We run fast through the rain as it blotches the sand.

Will Dad be there?

Don't stop.

I'm not . . . will Dad . . . ?

No.

But he said . . .

He said he could see it . . . he didn't say he was there.

Another flash of lightning.

1 2 3 4 5—

Shit!

The ground rumbles beneath us. The rain turns to ice.

Is it an earthshake?

An earthquake?

Yes.

No.

A tin hut lights up silver in the distance. We run up and down the path and then scramble inside. We put our hands on our knees, try to get our breath back as the rain drips off our hair onto our feet. We sit down on the bench. The hail falls like bullets on the roof as we dry our face and watch the storm cross the sea.

A lady with a black dog stumbles across the sand towards us.

Hide!

Where?

We slide along the bench and sit in the darkest corner.

The lady comes through the door, her face is red from running, her glasses are steamed from the rain. She puffs out her cheeks.

'Phew,' she says. 'We didn't see that coming, did we?'

We did.

Shush.

The lady smiles. 'Still, we can't complain, can we boy?' She bends down and pats her dog. 'Because it's been a wonderful summer.'

Has it?

!

313

Can't we talk to her?

No.

Because she's a stranger?

Yes.

And we don't trust strangers?

—

The lady turns around and looks at us.

'Oh,' she says. 'I didn't see you there.'

She takes off her glasses and wipes them on her blouse. We pull our bag and book towards us.

'Oh,' she says, 'very kind.'

The dog wags its tail, sniffs the ground, then our trainers. We hold out our hand.

Don't touch it.

But I like dogs.

I don't.

Hello . . . what's your name?

I said we don't talk to strangers.

But I'm talking to the dog.

!

What's your name?

The lady holds her glasses up to the light. 'Rufus,' she says. 'His name's Rufus.'

Don't touch—

We stroke the dog's head.

!

Hello Rufus.

The lady smiles. 'Not everyone likes dogs.'

I do.

I don't.

'Sorry?'

I do.

I don't.

The lady sits down on the bench, puts her glasses on and sees us for the first time.

'Oh . . . Oh . . . I thought there were two of . . . Rufus!' She slides her fingers through Rufus's collar and pulls him towards her.

We're looking for our dad.

'. . . Sorry?'

We're looking for our dad.

'Are you?'

Yes.

'Well . . .' She leans forward and looks out into the storm. 'I . . . I don't think I passed him.'

She doesn't want to talk to us.

We're writing a book.

!

This is our book. Tom did the writing, I did the pictures.

'Umm . . .'

The lady slides along the bench.

Because she needs the light to see?

Because we stink.

We slide towards her.

This is my picture.

!

315

Do you like it?

'It's . . . it's lovely.' She looks out of the door. 'Oh, look,' she says. 'I think the rain is stopping.'

It's not, it's still pouring. Do you like this one?

DAD COMING HOME

She slides further away and we follow until she is trapped in the corner.

Will you read it?

She shakes her head.

Will you read it? Beep.

She doesn't know about the beep.

Oh . . . it's what the Russians do in space.

'I've . . . I've not got any money.'

?

!

'I've not got any money.'

That's OK, neither have we.

Her eyes glisten behind her glasses.

We don't want your money.

Her hand shakes as she rolls back her sleeve.

'Here.'

Ten to ten?

We don't want your watch.

Ten past two?

We hold her wrist.

Is that the time in Russia or here?

'Please . . .'

Let go.

—

But she hasn't read Dad's letter—

Rufus barks.

We let go of her hand and search for one of Dad's letters.

Got one.

The lady stands up, backs away towards the door.

He sent it from the—

The lady turns and runs out into the rain.

—

—

I thought I told you not to talk to strangers.

But she wasn't strange.

Strangers and being strange aren't the same thing.

Oh . . . So the lady wasn't strange?

No.

And the lorry driver?

No.

And Reverend Franklin?

—

And Reverend Franklin?

No, he was strange.

We rest our head against the tin, close our eyes and remember all the strangers we used to count as we tried to get to sleep.

Mr Dobbs. Mrs Curtis. Mrs Jenkins. Mr Forster—

You don't have to count them now!

Aren't we going to sleep?

No, it's too early.

We look at the letter in our hand.

28th June 1971

Dear Tom. Dear Jack.

The sun is getting hotter. The moon is getting colder. I checked both of them this morning with my thermometer.

Tom, make a note of the readings, 6,000 degrees and minus 238.

Jack, here are the pictures I took. Sorry, Georgi has hidden the crayons.

Georgi says Ha!

Viktor tells him to stop laughing because he's using up all the oxygen. I can hold my breath...
....
.... for 2 minutes and 12 seconds.

Tom, write it down.

Jack, don't try it.

Love, Dad.

X

The wind whistles past the door and blows in the rain. The clouds hang low and black as the sun peeps out behind them and turns the sea silver.

We think about Dad and his letters, how we wished he'd sent more, how we wished we'd replied quicker.

And we think of Georgi and Viktor.

. . . Yes. We think about Georgi and Viktor and we are glad that Dad didn't go alone.

The ridges of the tin dig into our back. We pick up our book and wipe the rain off the cover and lie down.

Are we reading again?

There's nothing else to do.

We could play with my Lego.

We're too old.

!

—

Maybe we could get Meccano!

Maybe.

Can we get it tomorrow?

Yes.

If the sun comes out?

Yes, if the sun comes out.

Summer 1971

Dad always told us that we'd climbed the hill so many times we could do it blind. Me and Jack stood at the bottom and tied the ropes of our dressing gowns together so we wouldn't lose each other in the dark. I had the instructions in my pocket and a screwdriver and a spanner. Jack carried the torch and a hammer.

I'm scared.

You were scared.

No, I'm scared now.

Because of our story?

Because it's dark.

We turn off the torch to save the battery. Everything is black. The waves sound so loud they could be rushing around our feet.

Our head aches.

I know.

Do we need our—

No, we need water.

And food?

Yes.

Eggs and bacon?

———

Beans and toast?
You're making us hungry.
Fish and chips?
We'll find some in the morning.
Everything?
All those things.
We lean forward and hold our head.
To keep me in?
To stop it exploding.
Will it?
No.
But it feels like it?
Yes.

———

We shiver, wrap our jumper tight around us and wish we'd had enough space in our bag to pack the other two.
Ready?
Yes.
We turn the torch back on.

The washing machine and the fridge shone like car headlights in the dark. The dustbin lids and tyres were deep holes in the ground. Me and Jack walked round them and ducked under the radar scrambler. Wires trailed across the grass into the boxes and out again, just as Dad had drawn them in his diagram. We bent down, picked up the ends and wrapped them around our arms. The wind blew and a noise like a hundred owls hooting sounded across the site.

Jack stopped. I checked the sky for spies and satellites, but all I saw was the moon and a shooting star.

The hooting sounded again. Jack's eyes grew wide in the dark.

'It's just the poles,' I said. 'It's just the wind blowing across the poles.'

I unfolded Dad's instructions and we walked around inside the circle. Jack shouted out the parts. I ticked them off the list.

'Dustbin.'

'Check.'

'Hairdryer.'

'Check.'

'Electric fire.'

'Check.'

I put the list down. We were running out of time.

We picked up the wheels and the tyres, rolled them to the edge and pushed them off into the dark. We ran back to the launch site and untied our dressing gowns so we could work faster. I carried all the boxes and wires, Jack wheeled the lawnmower and the vacuum cleaner. Then we carried the spotlight together. It was so heavy that our arms ached when we got to the bottom. We wanted to stop and have a rest but we had to go back up for the petrol can. Dad said it was the most important thing, that it was pointless building a rocket if you didn't have any fuel to fly it. It was so important that he wrote the equation in white paint on the front of the can.

$$Fuel = W \times V \div D \text{ when } E = MC^2$$
$$\text{and } E \text{ is constant.}$$

We carried it down together, stopping every twenty strides so it wouldn't spill. We were as careful as we could be but we still stank of petrol when we got into bed in the middle of the night.

When I woke up in the morning the sky was blue in the middle, turning white and misty at the edges. The weatherman had said the mist would burn away during the day and that there would be no wind. Me and Jack got up, put our clothes on and ran out into the garden. All the rocket's parts were laid out on the grass just as we had left them. We looked at the sky, then looked at each other and smiled. It was a perfect day to build a rocket.

I found some wire in the shed and wrapped it around two posts. Jack found a piece of card and wrote a sign:

DANGER. LAUNCH SITE.
KEEP OUT.

Then we got the instructions and tried to put the launch site back together.

I put boxes on top of boxes and trailed wires across the ground. We put the washing machine drum under the radar scrambler and stacked the tyres on top. Then I got the petrol can and placed it in the shadow of the fridge.

We spent all morning and all afternoon moving things around and checking them with the diagram, checking the boxes, tracing the wires, but Dad had drawn so many arrows pointing in so many directions that we couldn't tell if we were holding the diagram the right way up or upside down. Where I had the tyres he had the washing machine, and where I had the washing machine he had the wheels. I tried moving them around inside my head but it still didn't make any sense. I couldn't find the rocket boosters or the stabilising struts and even if I had been able to find the red button to start the engines, I didn't have any nitrogen to cool them down.

It was T minus one hour, thirty minutes, twenty-five seconds and counting when we got two chairs from the kitchen and put them in the rocket.

I think we should stop now.
Why?
Because I'm tired.
But you're never tired.
Then I'm cold.
We hug ourself.
Better?
No.

——

The radar scrambler—

We haven't told them about the radio.

What?

We haven't told them about the radio.

I thought the rocket was more important.

I'll tell them.

!

We built a radio . . . a fox's radio.

A fox radio.

?

The radio didn't belong to a fox.

No, it belonged to us. I'll show them the diagram.

I think they've seen enough diagrams.

I'll have a look . . .

I think we should keep reading.

Do we have to?

But you always want to read.

I know.

What's wrong then?

. . . Nothing.

Are you bored?

No.

What then?

I just want our story to last longer.

Why?

Because . . .

Because?

Because this is the last bit before I die.

—

—

The radar scrambler glowed red as the sun went down behind our house. Jack pushed the vacuum cleaner around the launch site like he was sweeping for mines. Mum sat beside me on the back step while I checked the instructions for the last time. She nodded at our rocket.

'How long did it take you?' she asked.

'All day,' I said.

'And all night?' She smiled as she took a sip from a mug of coffee.

'Did we wake you up?'

'No,' she said. 'You have to go to sleep to wake up.'

'And you didn't sleep?'

'No,' she said.

Jack did a second sweep of the launch site.

'Were you thinking about Dad?'

'Yes . . . and . . .'

I waited for her to say something else but she just sat there staring, with her finger tracing a ring around the top of her mug.

I thought about the hottest summer, how it felt like she had been away almost as much as Dad. I thought about how much she must have missed him, that maybe she was lonely. Me and Jack always had each other and our letters, and we got to see him on the TV. All she had was a picture of Dad on the fridge, and Auntie Jean.

'Why didn't you watch him?' I asked.

She turned her head slowly towards me.

'Sorry?'

'Why didn't you watch Dad on TV?'

She smiled, but looked sad and tired.

'I did,' she said. 'I do . . . I watch him all the time.'

'But not on TV?'

She put her hand on my head and slid it down to my neck.

'No,' she said. 'Not on TV.'

She got up and went inside. I looked down at the instructions and followed the wires across the paper, out of the boxes, into the washing motor and then through the tyres until the line stopped at the edge of the page.

'Finished!' Jack shouted from the middle of the launch site.

It was T minus forty-six minutes, twenty-three seconds and counting. Me and Jack were almost ready to launch. All we needed was power.

I flipped the paper over, traced the wire across the page until it went into a big box with the words **Electricity Generator** written on it. I looked around the garden but none of the parts looked like a generator.

I thought of going into the house, connecting a wire under the stairs, but Fuel = W x V ÷ D when E = MC^2 and E is constant. I read it again. E must be constant . . . I needed maximum power that wouldn't cut out. I couldn't rely on our electrics, I couldn't rely on a power that might switch off in the middle of the launch just because Mum didn't have enough coins.

I picked my torch up off the step and walked the path along the back of the house.

'Where are you going?' Jack shouted.

'Looking for a generator,' I said.

'What's that?'

'Electricity,' I said.

I went into the shed and flashed the torch around. There were two brushes leaning against the wall and a grass box for the mower. I shone the torch further but there was nothing else except for my old bike and two motorcycle helmets. I picked them up and carried one under each arm.

'Jack,' I shouted.

I waited for Jack to answer but all I could hear was my breath and the buzz of insects. I stepped out of the shed and walked back into the garden. The moon was above me now, the launch site was a series of dark shapes that threw darker shadows across the ground.

'Jack!' I shouted. 'I've found us two helmets.'

He didn't reply.

I walked down through the garden and ducked under our launch-site sign. The clocks were still ticking, T minus twenty-eight minutes, thirty-three seconds and counting. The sound of metal scraping against metal echoed in the air. I shone the torch in the boxes, in the fridge and inside the drum of the washing machine.

'Jack?'

The sound grew louder. I walked under the radar scrambler, the foil brushed against my head and made me shiver. I looked around for Jack but all I could see was the vacuum cleaner in the middle of the garden with the flex trailing off into the dark. It twitched like a snake on the grass.

'Jack?'

I picked up the flex, ran it through my hands like I was a climber in a cave and followed it to the bottom of the garden where the grass turned to stingers. The flex twitched in my hands. I followed it to a ladder that was leaning against the fence over into Auntie Jean's garden. I looked up and saw Jack standing at the top, grinning, with the vacuum-cleaner plug in his hand.

'Jack,' I whispered, 'what are you doing?'

'I've found it.'

'What?'

'The electricity.' He nodded to a sign that was nailed to the fence.

'No, Jack,' I said.

'But the diagram says we need a generator.'

'I don't think Dad meant that.'

'Why not?'

'Because it says Danger – Keep Out . . . and we only need 600 volts, not 50,000.'

'But—'

The ladder started to wobble, Jack stepped off the top rung and sat on the top of the fence. I told him to be careful, said that he should come back down. He pointed at the generator.

'I can see our footballs,' he said.

I told him to leave them, that the man from the electricity board would throw them back when he came.

But I don't think he heard.

Because I could see our planes too.
I told you not to get them.
You didn't.
I did.
You said you wanted your Spitfire.
I said I could wait.
And your Commodore.
!
And——
That was different.
?
It was the only one I had.
——

Jack looked back at me, smiled and jumped down on the other side——

And we all lived happily ever after!
?
THE END!
What are you doing?
I want to stop now.
We can't, we have to tell everyone what happened.
But they all know that I die.

But they don't know how.

And that's important?

Yes.

For them?

For us.

?

It might be cathartic.

?

It might make us feel better.

It might help us complete the circle?

Yes.

Can't we just take pills?

They don't work.

But we could pretend . . .

———

I could just go to sleep.

———

And wake up again . . . Couldn't I?

No. We can't do that any more.

Do you want me to go away?

———

Do you want me to go away?

. . . No.

Then stop reading.

. . . I can't . . . Mum said I had to write everything,
Dr Smith said we had to read it all, that it would help
us understand . . .

Do I have to listen?

No.
We put our fingers in our ears.

Jack looked back at me, smiled and jumped down on the other side.

I can still hear you.
Sing then.
The grand old Duke of York, he had 10,000 men.

I told him to come back. He said he could see my Commodore. I told him to be careful but I could hear him on the other side, crunching his feet through the gravel.

'Got it,' he shouted.

'My Commodore?'

'. . . And my boomerang.'

My Commodore flew over the fence and landed behind me on the grass. The boomerang went towards the house, circled back and rattled the radar detector.

And when they were up they were up. And when they were down . . .

Jack went quiet. I asked him what was wrong. He mumbled something. I put my ear against the fence. Jack mumbled again.

'What is it, Jack? What's wrong?'

The hum of electricity droned through my head.

'Houston, I have a problem,' he said.

'Can't you find your plane?'

'No,' he said. 'I can't get back out.'

'Stay still,' I said. 'Don't touch anything. I'm coming over.'

The flex tugged tight in my hand.

'Jack, I said stay still.'

I held onto the ladder and put my foot on the bottom rung.

'Uh-oh.'

'What now?'

'Houston, there's another problem.'

'I know,' I said. 'You can't get out . . . I'm coming to get you.'

'No, it's not that,' he said. 'I can't find the plugger.'

'The plugger?'

'Where I put the plug . . .'

'No, Jack, don't touch the plugger.'

I climbed to the top of the ladder and looked over. A big grey lump of metal hummed like a monster in the dark. Jack knelt down in the gravel by a red light in the corner.

And when they were only halfway up . . .

'Jack, no!'

Jack reached out with the plug. The generator crackled. Sparks jumped out of it and into Jack's body. He glowed white in the middle and turned purple at the edges.

'Let go, Jack,' I shouted. 'Let go.'

His body shook. I tried to climb over the fence but my feet and hands were stuck like they were welded to the ladder.

334

The world lit up blue. Jack's eyes turned red. Sparks of electricity ran from his hands along the wire to the washing machine and back to the house. I heard a scream, a high-pitched scream that screeched through the middle of my head, and then a bang.

I fell through the air and landed on the ground. Everything was dark like someone had turned the lights out on the world. My head hurt, my feet and hands were numb. I opened my eyes, saw the stars and felt cold. And I lay there, just staring up with my chest going up and down and my breath smoking like a gun. I tried to stand but my legs were dead and my head was heavy. The ground was turning. I was turning. And the radar scrambler, the fridge and the washing machine were all spinning twice as fast like satellites around me. I knelt up, smelt burning.

Am I dead yet?

—

'Jack!'

He didn't reply. All I could hear was a crackle of electricity coming from the other side of the fence. I crawled down the garden and found the ladder all bent and twisted out of shape in the middle of the stingers.

'Jack!' I shouted again.

A loud crack sounded behind me.

I turned around, looked back up the garden. All the lights had gone out in our house. An orange flame flickered in the kitchen and smoke billowed out from under the back door. I bent under the wire and staggered through the launch site. The flame grew bigger. I jumped up the steps and looked inside. The cooker was burning, the ceiling was melting, little white bits of plastic dripped onto the table and the floor.

'Mum!' I shouted.

No answer.

I tried the handle but it was too hot to turn. I jumped down the steps and looked back down the garden. I thought of Jack lying there and how I didn't want to leave him alone in the dark. I wanted to run back to him. I wanted to find him laughing at me and playing with his planes. My heart was thudding, my legs wanted to run but I couldn't make up my mind which way to go. The glass cracked on the kitchen window. Smoke poured out. I thought of Mum choking inside. I ran around the side of the house, hammered my fist on the front door and shouted again. The air crunched with the sound of wood splitting and burning. I peered through the letter box and hoped I would see her running through the hall towards me, but all I saw was smoke and flames. I ran around the front of the house and looked in through the sitting-room window. Mum was lying on the settee, the TV was burning in the corner. I banged my fist on the glass. I think I saw her open her eyes, I think I saw her roll over, but it may have been a trick of the smoke in my mind.

Sirens echoed in my head and a thousand searchlights flashed across the front of my house as fire engines and ambulances drove into our road. I heard someone shout my name. Auntie Jean was standing on the path. I pointed in through the window.

A fireman ran past her, across our garden towards me, bent down, picked me up and ran. He said something but his voice was muffled by his mask. He put me down on the path. Auntie Jean shuffled towards me, one hand holding her dressing gown together, the other over her heart.

'Oh, Tom,' she said, 'have you seen Jack or your mum?'

I nodded, then shook my head. Auntie Jean looked at me like she didn't understand. I tried to speak, I tried to breathe, but my heart hurt and my tears were stuck in my throat. My mum was burning in the sitting room. My brother was dead in the garden. Auntie Jean put her hand on my shoulder.

'Don't worry, my love, I'm sure they'll be OK.'

I walked away from her, backwards up the hill, watched the smoke pour out of the windows, disappear up into the sky and cover the moon. I thought about Dad and wished he'd come home.

A fireman came out of our house with Mum across his shoulder. Two ambulance men met him on the path. They put her down, covered her face with a mask and wrapped her in blankets. My head flashed with lights and sirens and pictures of Jack. I heard voices calling but still I kept walking until I found myself running and the shouts turned to whispers.

At the top I sat down and cried as I watched our house burn.

———

———

———

—

Jack.

—

Are you OK?

—

Jack!

—

Chapter Seventeen

We sit on the sand dune and look down at the beach. Windbreaks flap, parents sleep on the sand and children run around in circles with buckets and spades.

We wish we could do that.

Don't we?

Don't we, Jack?

We wish we could be like sharks again.

We pick up our bag, slide down the dune and walk along the beach. The sand turns to pebbles and the pebbles turn to rocks until we reach pools of water, grey, like mercury reflecting the clouds.

Like mercury.

Like mercury, Jack. What's mercury, Tom? It's a metal that's a liquid. Is it? Oh.

How much longer?

How much longer are you going to sulk? It's not my fault . . . I didn't make our book up, I only wrote it down.

This is what happens every time we get to the last chapter of our book. One of us wants to keep reading, but one of us goes missing like Captain Scott. No . . . Captain Oates. Who, Tom? Captain Oates, Jack . . . I'm stepping outside . . . A giant step? Ha. No. I'm stepping outside and I may not be coming back. Is that what it said in your encyclopaedia? Yes . . . Well, it was something like that.

Still not talking?

We reach over for our bag and take out our book. We have to do what Dr Smith said, we have to write the last chapter, we have to complete the circle.
 The wind turns the pages, flips the loose pieces of paper, blows the newspaper cuttings out onto the wet sand.
 You should have stuck them in. I told you to stick them in.

A light flashes in the corner of our eye, then another and another. We look over our shoulder and squint, like when our torch catches us in the night.

Police?

I don't know.

We look back up the beach, beyond the dunes. Cars turn in car parks and reflect the sun. Our heart beats again.

We pick up the wet pieces of paper and peel them apart.

The Evening Gazette 6TH JUNE 1971

RUSSIANS BLAST INTO SPACE

The Evening Gazette 12TH JUNE 1971

RUSSIANS IN TROUBLE

The Evening Gazette 30TH JUNE 1971

RUSSIANS SUFFOCATE

The Evening Gazette 1ST JULY 1971

MOTHER AND BOY DIE IN HOME-MADE
ROCKET TRAGEDY

Our hands start to tremble as we read them over and over again, but the words turn to a blur as our eyes start to water and our throat starts to ache. We wish we could go back and change the headlines. We wish we could go back and change the whole of summer. But we can't change it. We can't change it just because people die . . . Can we?

Can we?

We wipe our tears on our arm, put the headlines under a rock and hope they will dry in the sun.

—

—

Do you want to draw?

You can draw your monster.

Last chance . . .

We shake our head and pick up our pen.

Do you want to write? We could write the last chapter. You can choose the title . . . Any ideas?

The Great Escape?

Ha!

A shadow creeps across the sand, blocks the sun from the page. We hear a hissing sound, like a snake breathing in and out. We keep our head down and hope that it will go away.

The hiss gets louder.

We look up. A boy stands in front of us with blue flippers on his feet and a pair of goggles on top of his head. He smiles as he pulls a snorkel out of his mouth.

'What are you doing?' he asks.

We look back down at our book, at our pen shaking in our hand.

'What are you doing?'

The flippers flap on the sand as the boy edges closer.

We're writing . . . We're reading our book.

'Oh . . . What's it about?'

Our dad.

He points towards the sea. 'Is that him?'

A man with a hairy back pulls a yellow dinghy between the waves.

No, that's not him.

The boy sits down on the rock beside us.

'Where is he then?'

He went away.

'Where to?'

Are you going to tell him?

The boy screws up his face.

Are you?

He went away. He went to a building on a hill.
'And did he come back?'
No.
We flick through the pages of our book.
'It's lots of words . . . Did you write them all?'
Yes.
'And draw all the pictures?'
No, my brother did that.
'What's his name?'
Jack.
'Is he here?'
Yes.
'I can't see him.'

Say hello.

'Is he shy?'
No, he's sulking.
The boy laughs.
'Which one is him?'
Sorry?
'Which one is him?' He taps his finger on a picture
of us sitting with Mum on the settee. 'Is that him?'
Yes.
'And is that you?'
Yes.

'Were you twins?'

——

——

'Were you——'

No. People just said we looked the same.

'Simon!' We turn around. The boy stands up. A man marches across the sand towards us. 'I told you, no.' He grabs the boy by the arm.

'But he's writ a book.'

'Has he?'

The man stares at us. We look back at our book.

——

'Are you OK?'

——

'Are you OK?'

Yes.

He bends down, puts his face level with ours and we hope he can't see what's inside.

'Are you sure?'

We nod.

Simon puts his snorkel in his mouth and starts to hiss again. The man holds his hand and they walk towards the sea. We lie back on the sand, rest our head on our bag. We think about Dad. We imagine him walking through the rock pools with his carrier bag.

We remember the marks on his body and on the side of his head. We lift our hand and run our fingers over ours; we remember the buzz, we remember the pain and I remember how it takes one of us away.

We open our book and read his last letter.

T PLUS 42 DAYS 22 HOURS 34 MINUTES 26 SECONDS AND
COUNTING . . .

Dear Jack. Dear Tom.

I'm sorry I've not written. I am tired.

Jack, I love your rockets, even when they go the wrong way.

Tom, keep writing your book, lots of people will read it soon.

I have to go.

The Russians are coming.

Tonight the sun will burn a hole through my head and in
the morning, when I wake up, everyone will be gone.

Love, Dad

X X X

We hear the whine of turbines turning. We look up and watch an aeroplane cross the sky.

A DC-9?

A DC-10.

How can you tell? It's got three lots of landing gear. Has it? Yes . . . and it's got a bigger engine, that's why it's louder, remember? Do you remember, Jack?

We look at our letter again. We wish it wasn't the last one. Sometimes we wondered whether Dad had kept writing, that there might be a pile of letters at the post office waiting for us to collect because they didn't know where we had moved. But now we know that didn't happen, we know this is the last letter, because one of us has worked it out, one of us knows what the letter means. We read it again. Tonight the sun will burn a hole through my head and in the morning, when I wake up, everyone will be gone . . .

The wind blows the sand, and the sand blows in our eyes. We hold the letter tight and bury our head in our arms. We know what Dad was telling us. Don't we?

We know that the sun that burnt through his head is the same as the electricity they want to buzz through ours.

We put our letter back in the book and pick up our pen. We close our eyes and listen to the aeroplane roar.

Chapter Eighteen

The sea has got bigger, the beach has got smaller, all the windbreaks have been taken down and all the children have gone. There is just us, two seagulls and the sound of the waves. We reach into our bag, take out our Spitfire and our Messerschmitt. We turn their propellers and check their guns, then fly them towards the water.

Bandits at six o'clock?

Bandits at twelve?

They climb into the red sky and fire their guns . . .
They bank left at the water's edge, turn again towards the dunes. They lose altitude, skim over castles and moats and land on the sand.

We pick up our book and put it on the sand next to our planes.

We take off our shirt and put it on top.

A wave creeps up the beach and covers our feet. We walk through the shallows, the water splashes up our legs, over our waist, makes us shiver as it stings the sunburn on our back. We fall forward. The water shoots up our nose, bubbles around our ears.

What are we doing?

Jack!

That's me!

!

We stand up, spit out the salt water and wipe it from our eyes.

Miss me?

—

Did you miss me? Beep.

. . . No, not really.

!

Ha!

So you did?

Just a little bit.

So what are we doing?

—

What are we doing? Beep.

Going in the water.

Because we're dirty?

—

Because we're dirty?

Because we have to.

Why?

——

Because of Mrs Unster?

——

Because we can't find Dad?

——

Because of Frost?
. . . Yes, all of those things.
The water splashes around our chest.
Are we going right under?
Yes.
Up to our neck?
Yes.
But I can't swim.
I can.
Will you teach me?
I'll try.

——

We lift our feet off the ground, swim beyond the breakers, into the swell where the water gets darker.
Can I stand up here?
No.
But I might die.

——

Will you save me?
I won't have to.
?
You can't die twice.

Oh.

We drop our feet and search for the bottom, but all we find are trails of seaweed and colder water. We kick our feet, swim, then cling to a buoy.

Are we giving up?

?

Are we giving up looking for Dad?

Yes.

Because we've reached the edge of the world?

Because everyone else has gone.

So we're not going back this time?

We can't.

Because I give us headaches.

Because . . .

?

Because they'll take you away.

But I always come back.

You won't. Not this time.

Buzz buzz?

Yes.

—

—

We kick our legs and look towards the horizon.

The place where the sea meets the sky?

The place where the sky meets the sea.

Is that where we're going?

—

It looks a long way.

—

Is it as far as the moon?
No. It's a mile away.
Did Dad tell you that?
No, I read it in a book.
Your encyclopaedia?
Yes.
Oh . . . What's after the horizon?
Beyond.
What's after the beyond?
What's beyond the horizon?

—

Ireland.
Will Dad be there?
I hope not.
Because it's cold?
Because the people are still fighting.
Oh . . . What's beyond Ireland?
America.
Is that a long way too?
3,100 miles.
Can we swim there?
No.
Because Dad won't be there either?
Because it's too far.
Can we swim to Russia?
No.
Why not?

Because it's the other way.

Shall we turn back then?

I said we can't.

What happens when we get to America?

We keep swimming.

Because Russia is beyond America?

Yes . . . eventually . . . if we keep going.

?

You know why.

Because the world is a circle, like the moon?

Yes.

The sea laps around our chin. We close our mouth, try to stop the water from pouring in.

I'm cold.

——

Isn't he coming?

Who?

Dr Smith. He told us to stay out of the water.

——

Isn't he coming?

No, not this time.

We take a new grip on the buoy, look back at the beach, watch the sand dunes turn from yellow to orange, watch the waves creep towards our bag and clothes and our book balanced on the rock.

We've left our book behind.

I know.

Can we get it?

No.
Why not?

—

But we have to write more.
We've written as much as we can.
Because we've run out of paper?
Because we've run out of words.
So is this the last chapter?
Yes.
And you've written the last line?
I'm just about to.
On the sea?
In our mind.
And we're not going back?

—

And they'll never catch us?
No, never.
Ha!
Ha!
Can I say goodbye?

—

Can I say goodbye? Beep.
Yes.

—

—

Now?
Yes.

—

—

Goodbye.
Goodbye.

—

—

We let go of the buoy and swim towards the sun.

Afterlife

Are we dead yet?

Umm...

!

Yes.

But we can still talk?

Yes.

And we can still write?

——

And we can still write? Beep.

I can.

So what are we doing now?

We have to thank all the people who helped us write our story.

Oh good.

We have to thank our author.

He's old and wrinkly but he thinks he's good looking.

——

Like a tortoise.

——

Like a tortoise. Beep.

No. Not really.

—

—

—

We've got to thank Max, and Lois, and Tallulah.
For putting up with him.
For putting up with us.

—

—

We're sorry.
Yes.
We're very very sorry.
But we're grateful.
Yes, we're very very grateful too.
And we have to thank Ben Grose.
For the wasp in the can.
For not saying much but what he did counted lots.
And for making sure we met Harriet.
And for being our mate.

—

—

But most of all we have to thank JBS.
Just been shot!
Jon Bentley-Smith.
We like JBS.
We really like JBS.
Everybody likes JBS.
Because he's a great editor.
And a great writer and a great friend.

But most of all because he's mad.
Like us. Ha!
Ha!
Ha!
!

——

——

——

——

Have we finished?
Nearly. Just a few more.
And then we'll play We spy?
!
And then we'll play We spy?
Our author would also like to thank:
Sally Gander, Carrie Etter.
Dom Fox
Brad Howarth
Max, again!
For being the first readers.
And telling him to keep going.
Dan Coleman
Penelope Price
Ray Offiah
For making three years bearable.
Bret Hardman
For the advice and early edit.
Richard Francis

For his guidance.

Nicola Barr

His agent.

His secret agent!

Thanks for the belief and the patience.

Dan Franklin

For his faith and enthusiasm.

And we've got to thank George.

George Wolfe.

Hoooowl!

Do you have to do that?

Ha!

!

—

Thanks George for helping us whisper.

And thanks to all the other friends our author bored because he couldn't stop talking about us.

—

—

—

And we have to thank the Delays — we love the Delays!

Thanks for 'Long Time Coming' and 'Winter's Memory of Summer'.

And Radiohead.

For all their music, but especially 'Last Flowers'.

And finally...

His mum and dad.

For taking ages to read it with a magnifying glass.

!

It's true.

It's rude.

Oh.

—

—

—

And now we're finished?

Yes.

—

—

I spy with our little eye something beginning with…

!

Can we?

Me first.

OK.

I spy with our little eye something beginning with H.

H?

H.

Ummmm…

—

Hell?

No. Heaven.

Phew!